"We—we thought you were dead," she whispered. "Don't you understand?"

"All I understand is that you forgot me in only a few short months. And your wonderful new fiancé knew all along I wasn't dead."

"No Rand, he told me—".

He seized her trembling shoulders, his face white with rage. "He knew, I tell you! I gave him a letter to give to you. Did you get a letter?"

"No, but there must be some mistake. Ben cried when he told me about how he found your body—"

"Yeah, I'm really dead, aren't I?".

"Bu–but Ben *saw* your body." She felt idiotic repeating herself, but her mind felt somehow sluggish and stupid. She couldn't seem to reconcile the two different stories.

"I tell you he knew all along I wasn't dead! He was with the troops who rescued me!"

"But we saw in the paper—"

"It was wrong and he knew it was wrong. And how do you explain the letter he neglected to give you?"

Her green eyes grew huge in her white face as she suddenly grasped the enormity of Ben's treachery. What a fool she'd been! How gullible she was! All that phony sympathy—and the details he'd offered to prove to her Rand was really dead! "But we didn't know! How can you blame me for it?"

COLLEEN COBLE is a church secretary in Wabash, Indiana—the setting for her first book. She and her husband are restoring an old home while they wait for their grown children to give them grandchildren. Colleen's favorite thing is people, she loves them all.

Where Leads
the Heart

Colleen Coble

𝓗𝓮𝓪𝓻𝓽𝓼𝓸𝓷𝓰 𝓟𝓻𝓮𝓼𝓮𝓷𝓽𝓼

In memory of my brother, Randy Rhoads,
who taught me to love the mountains of Wyoming
and
my grandparents, Everett and Eileen Everroad,
who loved me unconditionally.
May you walk those heavenly mountains with joy.

A note from the author:
*I love to hear from my readers! You may correspond with me
by writing:* **Colleen Coble**
Author Relations
PO Box 719
Uhrichsville, OH 44683

ISBN 1-57748-312-X

WHERE LEADS THE HEART

All of the characters and events in this book are fictitious. Any
resemblance to actual persons, living or dead, or to actual events
is purely coincidental.

Cover illustration by Chris Cocozza.

PRINTED IN THE U.S.A.

one

"Well, I think it's just disgraceful." Anne Drake sniffed behind her lace handkerchief and rearranged the folds of her long skirt as she sat against the wall on a crude wooden chair. Above her head hung an assortment of bridles and farm implements. Her foot tapped in time to the music as her pale blue eyes followed Sarah Montgomery's figure around the floor. She perched her glass of iced tea on a weather-gray wooden barrel, then turned to watch the dipping couples. "First she snatches Rand out from under poor Sally's nose, and now she's taken up with Ben Croftner—with Rand scarcely a year in his grave."

Her companion, Nora Cromwell, nodded, twisting her thin, colorless lips into the semblance of a smile. "I've never understood why all the fellows are attracted to her, anyway. That mass of hair—it looks quite messy most of the time. And those eyes—I declare, they put me in mind of a cat. That shade of green is quite peculiar." Nora's own eyes were a muddy, unremarkable brown, but she would have been mortified if anyone guessed her spitefulness held more than a trace of envy.

"It's probably all Ben's money." Anne sniffed again, the lines of petulance and discontent deepening around her eyes as she saw the way Sarah's hair caught the light from the dozens of lanterns strung around the barn.

Sarah couldn't help noticing the spiteful looks the young women kept sending her way as she whirled around the barn floor on Ben's arm, but she was used to it by now. Ever since she'd become engaged to Rand Campbell, the best-looking bachelor in the county, she'd been subjected to gossip and tittle-tattle behind her back. But it hurt just the same—

especially on top of the anguish of losing Rand a year ago.

Rand. Just the thought of him still brought almost unendurable pain, and she steered her thoughts away from the painful past. It was over and done with and no amount of wishing or crying would ever bring him back. *Will I ever get over his death?* she wondered.

She felt Ben tighten his grip around her waist as if he sensed her sadness and discontent, and she forced the fake, brittle smile to her face again. She wondered fleetingly if her face would crack before she could murmur her apologies and go home. It seemed that all the entire county of Wabash had done in the past few weeks was party. The dreadful Civil War was finally over and the Union was preserved, but at what a price. Scarcely a family in the county had been spared the loss of one of their loved ones. And she had lost the only man she had ever loved. She had tried all evening to find a last remnant of her old gaiety and join in the festivities, but it was just a mask.

Ben tightened his grip on her slender waist as the song ended and she tried to pull away. "Come outside a minute. I want to talk to you." His firm voice brooked no objection as he pulled her toward the big sliding door at the front of the barn, past the wooden tables piled high with cakes and pies of every imaginable flavor, past the rows of seated older women who watched their exit with tolerant, reminiscent smiles.

Sarah fought the feeling of impending doom that rushed up into her throat at his words. *He's going to ask me tonight,* she thought in panic. *I'm not ready yet.* Her steps faltered as she hung back. "Le—let me get my shawl." Her hands shaking, she grabbed her blue shawl from a peg on the wall and threw it over her shoulders.

"Come on." His voice impatient, Ben tugged on her arm and drew her outside into the crisp autumn air. The sunset was still a faint pink glow in the darkness, but the most light came from the lanterns strung around the graying barn and through the muddy yard. They swung in the light breeze, their lights dipping and swaying like some giant form of firefly. The air was moist and tangy, a mixture of ripening grain and the smoke from a bonfire in the adjoining field. The September night had a slight chill, and Sarah pulled her shawl more closely about her shoulders.

Ben pulled Sarah down onto a wooden bench away from the rest of the couples who watched the fire shoot sparks high into the dark sky. His eyes were dark, unreadable pools in the moonlight, but his voice was tender and earnest. "It's time we talked about our future, Sarah." He hesitated as if gauging her reaction. "I want to marry you. You know how I've felt about you for years, and now that Rand's gone—well, you need to get on with your life."

Sarah raised a trembling hand to her throat and felt her pulse fluttering under her fingertips. *No, I can't marry you,* she wanted to scream. *I still love Rand.* But the words stuck in her throat. She had to marry Ben. She'd watched her father's health go downhill ever since the news of Rand's death came. Wade said it was because their father was so worried about her future. He said she owed it to Papa to get her life settled, and she could see the sense of her older brother's words. How could she be selfish enough to refuse to do whatever it took to get Papa better? And besides, what else did the future hold except to be someone's wife?

She took a deep breath and said woodenly, "All right. I'll marry you." She winced inwardly at the flat tone of her voice.

Ben's smile of self-satisfaction deepened in spite of her less than enthusiastic response. "Wade assured me you'd be agreeable. I'm so glad, my dear. You won't be sorry."

I already am, she thought, her stomach sinking as she twisted her icy hands in the folds of her skirt. *I already am.*

"Let's go announce our good news." He drew her up and tucked her hand into the crook of his elbow. "Your family will be so pleased."

She pinned the smile back on her face as they walked into

the barn. Ben pulled her with him to the front of the room and waved his hands. "Ladies and gentlemen, may I have your attention?"

The music stopped with a last, dying squeal of the fiddle, and the flushed couples stared at them. Sarah felt the heat in her cheeks and took a deep, calming breath. She caught Amelia's horrified look and smiled encouragingly. Her best friend, Amelia, had been trying to talk her into defying Wade for weeks now. She seemed to dislike Ben for some reason.

Sarah glanced up at Ben and straightened her shoulders a little in pride. He was certainly very good-looking, but in a different way than Rand had been. Ben's hair was very blond, almost white, and he had gray eyes the color of the Wabash River on a stormy day. His pride at his own accomplishments gave him a self-confident, almost arrogant stature, and his self-assurance smoothed most obstacles he encountered. Like Wade said, she would never want for anything as Ben's wife. *Except for love,* an insistent voice whispered.

"You all know how long I've tried to get Sarah to agree to be my wife." Ben's voice interrupted her thoughts.

"I always thought she showed a lot of sense," called Jason Maxwell from up in the haymow where a group of young men had been playing checkers. A group of adolescent boys lounging in the hay of the loft as they watched the game hooted with laughter.

Ben laughed, too, but there was no humor in the look he threw Jason. "Well, you can all congratulate me—she finally gave in! You're all invited to the wedding—and it'll be a humdinger!"

Their friends and neighbors crowded up quickly to congratulate them, and Sarah was hugged and kissed as she fought to keep her smile from slipping. She saw Wade's complacent grin and the smile on her father's face. Then over her father's stooped shoulder, she saw the two Campbell boys, Rand's brothers. Her face whitened, and she pulled her arm out of

Ben's possessive grasp. She needed to talk to them in private, so she hurried to intercept them.

They stopped beside the heavily laden tables and waited for her. Jacob was home on leave for about a month. He had to report for duty at Fort Laramie about a week from now, after his own wedding to Sarah's friend, Amelia. Jacob took her hand, his dark eyes, so like his older brother's, sad in spite of his smile. "No need to worry, Sarah. We saw it coming. And Rand wouldn't want you to grieve forever. We just want you to be happy. Right, Shane?"

Shane, the youngest, pushed his blond hair out of his face and turned sober blue eyes on her. "Ri–right. The only thing is—" He hesitated and looked from Jacob to Sarah. "What if Rand's not really dead?"

Sarah gasped, her green eyes enormous in her pale face. "What do you mean?" She looked from one to the other in shock, unable to still the small, faint flutter of hope. Did they know something they hadn't told her? "What does he mean, Jake? Ben saw his body in the prison camp. We got official notification from the army, and his name was on the list in the newspaper."

"But we never got his body or his things," Shane insisted stubbornly. "There could still be some mistake. Maybe he was wounded real bad. Ben could be wrong."

"Shane, it's been over a year since he was reported dead!" Jacob said. "Don't you think Rand would have written or the army would have contacted us? Thousands died with no one to mark their graves or send their belongings home, both Union and Rebs. I know—I was there, too. Rand is dead!"

Tears welled up in Shane's eyes, and Sarah fought the ones shimmering on her own lashes as that glimmer of hope died. She didn't think she would ever get used to the reality of Rand's death, but she understood why Jacob was being so brutal. Shane couldn't begin to heal until he accepted it. Just as she was finally beginning to accept it.

Jacob threw a comforting arm around Shane's shoulders as tears trickled down the youngster's cheeks. "I'm sorry, Sarah," he said. "I had no idea such a notion was brewing in that brain of his. Forget what he said and just be happy." He reached out and touched one pale cheek. "Ben's a lucky guy. But remember, you'll always be a part of us, too."

"I'll remember," she whispered as she watched them thread their way through the throng. How she still loved Rand! Would the pain never go away? Every time she closed her eyes she could see his square-jawed face with its deep dimples. The warm brown eyes so alight with joy and love of life, the thick dark hair that fell heavily across his broad forehead. And he had been the kindest man she'd ever known. She'd helped him take food to needy families many times, and once he'd even given his new coat to a drunk shivering in just a ragged shirt. It was such a huge, tragic mistake for him to be lying in an unmarked grave somewhere.

There was a soft touch on her arm, and she whirled, afraid it was Ben, that he would see her tears and demand to know why she was crying. But it was just Amelia, her dark blue eyes anxious. "Amelia! No, don't say it," Sarah interrupted her friend's beginning protest. "I know you don't approve, but I really didn't have a choice."

Amelia McCallister sighed and tears hung on her long lashes. "Yes, you do. Can you look me in the eyes and tell me you love him?" She stared down into Sarah's defiant green eyes.

Sarah bit her lip in frustration. Amelia always cut right through to the heart of the matter. "N–no. Not like Rand. But I'll be a good wife to him. I have to marry someone, and Ben loves me." The excuses sounded weak, even to her own ears. "I have to get on with my life. It may not be the life I'd dreamed of or hoped for, but Ben will make sure it's a secure one."

Amelia hesitated, eyeing her friend. "I just don't trust Ben," she said finally. "I know I should, and it shames me I feel like that. I've prayed and prayed for more patience and compassion for him, but I just don't think he's all he seems."

"Well, you're the only one who seems to feel like that. Since he's gotten back from the war, everyone seems to think he's just wonderful." Sarah smiled and nodded toward the cluster of young ladies hovering around Ben in the middle of the floor. "I know a couple of girls who would give anything to be in my shoes. You must not have seen all the nasty looks flung my way tonight."

Amelia followed her gaze and gave a sigh. "They're just a little jealous," she said gently. "They haven't found the one God has for them yet. Why can't you wait for the right person?"

"You mean like Rand? There won't be that kind of love for me ever again. Anything will just be second best. Be happy for me, Amelia. Please?" Her heart-shaped face was irresistible when she smiled like that. "Be my bridesmaid?"

Amelia sighed in defeat. "You know I will if we're still here. When is the wedding?"

"We haven't set a date yet, but it probably won't be for a while. Don't worry—you'll still be the first bride." Sarah didn't know how she could stand to be separated from her best friend. She saw Ben motion with an imperious gesture. "I've got to go, but I'll let you know. We'll get together tomorrow and make some plans." She hurried off, pinning her smile back in place and wishing for the evening to be over. But now they'd have to stay for hours yet and accept everyone's congratulations.

By the time all the well-wishing and hugging were over, the rest of Sarah's family had left to go home. She'd hoped they'd all be in bed by the time Ben dropped her off, but a dim light still shone through the parlor window's lace curtains as he helped her down off the buggy. The parlor window was open, and she could smell the aroma of fresh brewed coffee. Evidently no one was planning on going to bed any time soon.

"You've made me very happy tonight, my dear," Ben said

as he leaned down to kiss her.

She couldn't help the involuntary flinch as he bent his head, but she forced herself to accept his kiss. *I'd better get used to it,* she thought in resignation.

Ben was aware of her recoil, and his grasp tightened around her waist as he frowned slightly.

In spite of her resolve, Sarah quickly pulled away from his possessive grip. "I'd better go in. I'll see you tomorrow." She rushed up the steps without waiting for a reply, her heart lightening with every step she took away from Ben.

He watched through narrowed eyes as she lifted her skirts and stepped up onto the wide front porch.

The speculation in Ben's eyes frightened Sarah a little when she looked back. He looked almost, well, evil, she thought with a shiver as she dragged her eyes from his strange gaze and hurried inside.

She heard the murmur of voices as she stepped into the hallway and sighed in resignation. She hung her shawl on a hook on the wall and walked into the parlor. The thick rug muffled her footsteps, but Wade looked up from his seat in the overstuffed chintz chair beside the fireplace as she entered. Her father lay on the matching sofa, his breathing labored and his face pale in the dying light from the fireplace. "Papa, are you all right? Should I call Doc Seth?" She rushed to his side, her heart pounding.

"No, no. I'm fine. Just tired." William's breathing eased as he smiled up at his beloved Sarah. He took her hand and drew her into an embrace. "You remind me so much of your mama tonight, Sweetheart. Her hair was the exact same shade as yours the night I met her. And her eyes—just like yours. I had a marble I kept for years because it was just like her eyes— deep emerald with gold flecks." He closed his eyes as much from the pain of memory as from the pain in his chest. "I just realized how much I'm going to miss you. It will be almost like losing your mama again."

Sarah's heart thumped in sudden hope. Could Wade be wrong about how Papa felt? "I don't have to get married, you know. I'd rather stay home with you and Joel, anyway." She was the only mother her young brother had ever known. Their mother, Kate, had died giving birth to Joel. She didn't know how either of them could bear to be separated.

But her father's words dashed her hopes. "No, no, Sweetheart. You've been too self-sacrificing already, and I should never have been selfish enough to let you. You were only eight when your mama died and much too young to take over the household and the new baby the way you did. I should have hired someone." He wiped a shaking hand across his brow, beaded with drops of sweat. "But I just wasn't thinking clearly. And all these years you've managed our home like a grown woman. It's time for you to step out on your own and have your own life, your own home." He sat up and swung his legs off the couch. "You get on up to bed now. That's where I'm headed."

Relieved at the way his voice seemed stronger, Sarah stood up as Rachel, Wade's wife, came into the parlor carrying a tray laden with cups of steaming coffee. "Here. Let me take that. It's much too heavy for you in your condition." Sarah eyed the gentle bulge under Rachel's skirt.

Rachel handed it over with a tired smile of thanks and a glance at her husband.

As if aware of the censorious look his wife gave him, Wade's gaze sharpened, and he smiled at his sister. A self-satisfied smirk. "I'm glad to see you came to your senses. Ben is quite a catch. Just see you don't forget your family when you're rich."

Was money all he ever thought about? Sarah bit back her angry words. She didn't want to upset her father. "That's not important," she said in a quiet voice.

Wade gave a cynical laugh. "It's the only thing that's important. I always thought you could do better than Campbell."

William saw the stormy light in Sarah's eyes and the angry color in her cheeks and laid a placating hand on her arm. "Why don't you go on up to bed, Sweetheart? You can tell us all about your plans tomorrow."

The battle light died in her eyes, and she nodded wearily. It didn't do any good to argue with Wade anyway. He had never liked Rand, probably because he was one of the few people Wade couldn't dominate. Rand had been a strong man, in body as well as spirit. She kissed her father good night and walked upstairs, running her hand along the smooth oak banister. She looked back down into the entryway as she thought about her father's words. She was going to miss her home more than she'd realized.

Once in the sanctuary of her room, she pulled off her dress and reached for her nightgown. She caught a glimpse of herself in the oval oak mirror. Goodness, but she'd lost weight in this past year! Her ribs were prominent stair steps up her chest, and her neck looked positively bony. She'd always been tiny, barely five feet tall, but now she looked as though a strong wind would blow her away. But grief had honed her beauty and chiseled the fine bones in her face. Her startling green eyes were enormous and stood out in sharp contrast to the honey golden skin stretched over her high cheekbones.

She looked around her familiar bedroom. The large room was furnished with dainty white furniture stenciled with pink. A lacy coverlet topped the feather bed, and dozens of pastel pillows offered a plump, safe haven to curl up and read. She pulled the coverlet back and crawled beneath the smooth sheets, pulling her feather comforter up to her chin. She was filled with a strange foreboding as Shane's words came back to haunt her. What if Rand wasn't dead? *That's just foolishness,* she told herself. She'd indulged in such daydreams in the first months after his death. But the feeling persisted as she drifted off to sleep.

two

Ben swung off his horse and walked quickly toward the house. Ever since yesterday's party, he'd been filled with a feeling of complacency and self-satisfaction. As he approached the stately brick two-story, he was struck again with his usual sense of pride in all he'd accomplished. He, Ben Croftner, son of the good-for-nothing drifter, Max Croftner, had pulled himself up by his own boot straps out of the dirt and lived in a house that was the envy of everyone in Wabash—and Indiana, for that matter. And if some of his business dealings didn't bear close scrutiny, well, that's just the way it was in the world of high finance. You did what you had to do to get to the top. There had been much opportunity since the war, and he had discovered he had an aptitude for exploiting it. And now Sarah was finally his.

He wiped his dusty shoes on the rug by the door, then stepped into the parlor. His pride rose again as he saw the elegant appointments in the front parlor. Velvet drapes, fine walnut tables and Dresden figurines, a plush rug imported from France, and an overstuffed horsehair sofa and chair. He frowned as he saw the figure on the sofa. Too bad he couldn't just leave his family behind the same way he'd left his old life. Although his brother *had* been useful this past year.

Labe swung around at his entrance and jumped up, an envelope clutched in his hand. "I ain't goin' to do it no more, Ben." His voice quivered with fear and outrage as he thrust the envelope into his brother's hand. "My boss almost caught me takin' it. And I ain't goin' to jail for nobody. Not even you."

Ben's contented smile softened the lines of petulance and selfishness around his mouth as he patted Labe's shoulder.

"You don't have to do it anymore. Sarah finally gave in last night. By the time the next letter comes, she'll be my wife."

Labe's mouth dropped open in disbelief. "I never thought you'd really pull it off. When you come back from the war with that crazy scheme, I thought fightin' them Rebs had done made you loco."

Ben's grin widened as he sank into the plushness of the high-backed chair and took off his sweat-stained Stetson and wiped his face. His voice grew soft with reminiscence. "When I got back and found out they all thought Rand was dead, I knew it would be an easy matter to let them go on thinking it. All I had to do was burn the letter I was supposed to give Sarah from Rand. Lucky for me I had such a faithful brother working in the post office." His gray eyes glinted with avarice. "I always knew she belonged to me."

"Easy for you, maybe," Labe burst out, his anger resurfacing at Ben's lack of thanks for all he'd gone through. "You're not the one who had to steal six letters with a boss like mine around. That Jack don't miss nothing that goes on. I don't see how I got away with it this long."

"I know, Labe, and I appreciate all you've done." A note of impatience crept into Ben's voice. "Like I said, it's all over. Now all you have to do is keep your mouth shut." He dismissed his brother's worries and looked at the envelope in his lap. "I suppose I should read what this says." He grinned as he ripped open the top and took out the single sheet of paper. "Won't Mr. High and Mighty Rand Campbell be surprised when he gets back and finds out Sarah is married to me!"

He settled more comfortably in his chair and quickly scanned the sprawling lines. His smile faded and a scowl twisted his handsome face. "He's coming home in a couple of weeks!" He ripped the page to shreds and jumped to his feet. "But he's going to be too late!" He strode out the door without another word to Labe.

Labe stared after him with growing dismay. If Rand came

home, how was he going to explain the missing letters? Why hadn't he thought of that before? Labe was not the brightest man in town, but he knew when he was in real trouble. He moaned low in his throat. Why'd he ever listen to Ben? "Ben's just a user," he muttered to himself as he watched Ben through the window. "Too bad most folks can't see past his good looks to the rottenness underneath."

"Just like Rand Campbell to spoil things," Ben muttered as he strode toward the barn. "But he's going to be too late this time." He flung the harness over his horse's still-damp neck and hitched up the buggy. As he flicked the buggy whip over the horse's head and headed toward the Montgomery farm, his narrowed eyes glittered with determination. He'd come this close—he wasn't about to let it all slip away now. Not even if it meant Rand really had to die.

He hadn't kept up a charade for five months to lose Sarah now. He'd been really clever, telling her how he'd found Rand in the prison camp and got him to the hospital, only to see him die while holding his hand. And Rand *should* have died. He'd been just a shell of a man with his skin stretched over his bones when he was finally liberated from Andersonville prison camp. It was the most hideous thing Ben had ever seen. But he had rallied, much to Ben's dismay. Ben really hadn't expected him to recuperate as fast as he had, and now he threatened to spoil all Ben's carefully laid plans.

Sarah was sweeping the front porch when he stepped down out of the buggy. She looked up with a start, afraid for an instant it was Wade back from the fields. That was one good thing about getting married, she thought. She'd get out from under Wade's thumb. She relaxed and lifted a hand in greeting when she saw him. How good-looking he was, she thought. His blond hair just curled over his collar, and his gray eyes were gentle and tender. She dispelled her misgivings from the night before. The strange look was just a trick of the moonlight. She was doing the right thing.

"How's my lovely lady today?" Ben bounded up the steps with a smile and took her hand, his anger carefully masked.

"A little tired," she admitted. "Everyone has been stopping by to congratulate me. News travels fast."

"Especially good news." He guided her down onto the porch steps and sat beside her. "I was talking to Labe this morning, and he was saying how good it would be to have a real woman doing for us once you and I are married. You know we haven't decided on a date yet, and I was hopin' to make it on my birthday next weekend. Could you be ready?"

"Bu–but Ben! That's only eight days." Panic rose in her throat, and she tried to keep the dismay out of her face as she stared at him. "There's such a lot to do. I–I have to make my dress. And—"

He gripped her shoulders and a note of impatience crept into his voice as he stared into her green eyes. "You can be ready, I'm sure. If you really want to be. Don't you think you've made me wait long enough? I surely don't care what you wear. Your Sunday dress will do just fine."

She dropped her eyes, ashamed. Why did he always make her feel so guilty, so indebted to him? "I can be ready," she whispered. She allowed his hug, then watched him ride away with something that felt like relief. What difference did it really make anyway? One date was as good as another if she was really going to go through with it, she thought as she squashed her misgivings. And besides, if she wanted Amelia to be her bridesmaid, the wedding needed to be before Amelia left.

She untied her apron and started toward the McCallister farm. She paused at the knoll overlooking Amelia's home. It was so pretty from up here. Doctor Seth and his family still lived in the log home he'd built when he first arrived twenty years ago, although with his burgeoning practice he could well afford an elaborate home in town. But she was glad the McCallisters had never moved. It was her second home, and she ran over the meadow that separated the two properties nearly every day.

The house had been added onto over the years and now sprawled carelessly in several directions. Their two families had been best friends ever since Sarah could remember. At one time there was hope that Amelia would marry Wade, but that was soon dashed as Wade grew to manhood and became the arrogant, self-righteous boor he was. Amelia felt sorry for him, but she had never had any romantic interest in anyone but Jacob Campbell.

Amelia was on the wide front porch, churning butter. "I was just coming to see you as soon as I was finished," she said, smiling, her face flushed with exertion. Tendrils of dark hair clung in curls around her face. "I have some ideas for the wedding."

Her smile faded as Sarah explained Ben's plans. "Eight days! Isn't that too soon to get everything ready?" she asked hopefully. "And you said I would be the first bride."

"It has to be enough time, and if we wait until after your wedding, you might have to leave too soon." Sarah avoided her gaze. "Ben wants to be married on his birthday. It's the least I can do after all I've put him through these past five months. You know how patient with me he's been—" Her voice faltered as she saw the skeptical look Amelia threw her way. She shrugged. "What difference does it make?"

"I suppose you're right," Amelia said slowly. "One time is as good as another to ruin your life. And I've never understood why you think you owe Ben anything. He hasn't done anything special for you. He was just determined to capture you, and it seems like he has."

"Don't start, Amelia. Please." Sarah's tone was uncharacteristically sharp, and she saw Amelia's blue eyes glisten with quick tears. "I'm sorry." She hugged her friend. "It's just that I have to go through with it. Papa would be so disappointed. And besides." She gave Amelia a wink. "I was thinking last night how nice it will be to get away from Wade."

Amelia smiled and blinked away her tears. "He just needs the Lord in his life."

Sarah just smiled. She was a little envious of her friend's faith. No matter what happened, Amelia seemed to trust God. She never had a bad word to say about anyone.

That's why her attitude toward Ben was so perplexing. Sarah knew her friend was just concerned. But really, this was for the best if Amelia could just see it. Sarah would make a fresh start with Ben, and as the years passed and she had children to occupy her time, maybe she could numb the pain in her heart.

❧

The next few days sped by as Sarah threw herself into marriage preparations. She fell into bed at night too exhausted to think or even to dream. Papa had bought her a new machine called a Singer treadle sewing machine. Her dress, even with its yards and yards of soft, creamy lace, quickly took shape under its whirring needle.

Friday afternoon she sat back and massaged her aching neck thankfully. It was finally finished. She stared out the living room window at the weeping willows swaying along the riverbank. The soft breeze, laden with the rich scent of the Wabash River, blew through the sheer curtains and caressed her flushed face. Unbidden, a memory of walking hand-in-hand with Rand along the riverbank hit her, and she clutched her skirt in anguish. *I won't think about him any more,* she told herself. *I'll be Mrs. Ben Croftner in two days.* Then all the ghosts would be laid to rest.

She jumped nervously as the knocker on the front door clattered. She jumped up and hurried to the front hall. Pastor Aaron Stevens stood on the front porch, turning his hat in his hands. "Pastor," she said in delight. "Come in."

"I was out calling on the new family by the river, the Longs, and just thought I'd stop in and see how you're doing," he explained as he followed her into the parlor. His deep blue eyes were concerned as he noticed her pallor and the dark circles under her eyes.

"I just finished my dress." She pointed to the heap of cream material on the sewing machine.

"Are you all right, Sarah? You look—" He hesitated as he sat down on the sofa. "Well, troubled. Not quite the picture of a joyous bride-to-be I expected."

She smiled wearily. Pastor always seemed able to sense her moods in a strange way. She sighed and nodded. "I guess I am troubled. More than I've admitted to anyone else. And I don't *want* to be! This is for the best—I'm sure of it."

Pastor Stevens pushed his heavy black hair away from his forehead. "Are you *really* sure about this marriage, little sister? Have you prayed about it?"

Sarah lifted her chin mutinously. "Not really. And I know you're going to say I should. But God didn't seem to be listening all those months when I prayed for Rand's safety." There. She'd finally admitted the thought that had been nagging her for over a year. Did God really care about her?

Pastor Stevens frowned as he leaned forward. "I had a feeling you blamed God for Rand's death. I'm glad you're finally admitting it." He took her hand, his dark blue eyes warm with concern and compassion. "Sarah, please listen to me. It's hard, I know, but we can't always see God's plan in our lives. I remember when I was a little boy, I was lying on the floor at my grandmother's feet. She was doing some embroidery work and I looked up at the underside of the hoop. The yarn was all tangled and gnarled. A real mess. But when I climbed up beside her and looked down at what she was working on, it was a beautiful garden. That's the way our lives are. We're looking at the picture from underneath, but God is working out a specific plan from above."

"No plan could be right without Rand in it! I don't think God really cares about me anymore." She didn't care if the words shocked Pastor, it was how she really felt. If God really cared, He wouldn't let her go through this heartache.

Pastor Stevens got up and knelt beside Sarah's chair. "God still loves you, Sarah. He didn't promise we'd never have trouble or heartache. In fact, He assured us we would. But He's given us His Word to go with us every step of the way. Can't you just trust Him like you used to? I remember the old Sarah and how she believed God for every little thing in her life. Wouldn't you like to be that same young woman again?"

"I just can't!" she said, standing up and moving to the window, her back to the young pastor. "Maybe someday when the wounds aren't still so fresh, I'll be able to trust Him like I should. But nothing has turned out like I expected. Every time I see the knoll on the other side of the woods, I remember it's the spot where Rand and I meant to build our home. Everywhere I look there are reminders of how my life is in shambles." She turned abruptly. "If you don't mind, Pastor, I have a lot of things to finish up." She knew she sounded abrupt and rude, but she just couldn't talk about it anymore. It hurt too much.

Pastor Stevens stood reluctantly, frustration etched on his face. "If you need to talk, you know where to find me," he said as he left. "Please pray about this before you go through with it, Sarah."

She didn't answer him, and he left after gazing at her for a moment. She breathed a sigh of relief when she heard the front door shut. She pushed away a stab of guilt as she went to the kitchen to start supper. She'd chosen her course, and she'd stick with it.

three

The train shrieked a warning of imminent arrival, and Rand
Campbell jerked awake, his heart pounding. He licked dry
lips—how he'd love a drink of his ma's iced tea. The thought
of sun tea brewing in a glass jug on the back step at home
caused a fresh wave of homesickness to wash over him. It
wouldn't be long, though.

Then the fear he'd tried to keep at bay for the past three
days flooded back. What would he find at home? He'd passed
mile after mile of war-ravaged scenes. Homes burned, fences
torn down, hopeless looks on the faces of women and children. What if he arrived and found his home gone and his
family missing? And Sarah. What if she were dead? *What if
she didn't wait for you?* a part of his mind whispered. He
pushed the thought away impatiently. His Sarah would wait
no matter what. *Then why didn't she write? Why didn't Ma
write?* The unanswered questions made him feel sick.

The train whistle blew again, and he peered out the soot-
streaked window. He was almost home; eagerly, he scanned the
rolling pastures outside the window. There was the Johnson
place; it looked as neat and well tended as usual. The Larsen
farm looked unharmed. The train slowed as it began its descent
into the valley. Through clearings in the lush canopy of glowing leaves, he could see the sparkling river and the town just
beyond.

The town of Wabash nestled between two steep hills, with
the courthouse on the far hill overlooking the sprawling brick
and wood buildings that clustered neatly below it. He drank
in the familiar buildings and the glimmer of water that ran in
front of the town like a silver ribbon. During the heyday of

the Wabash-Erie Canals, the river bustled with boats of all types and sizes, but since the railroad came, the canal traffic slacked off, and the river once again resumed its placid course. Hungrily he watched for a familiar face. But the streets and boardwalks were almost deserted. The few people he saw hurrying along were strangers.

But the town looked just the same. The ravages the war had left behind seemed very far away from this peaceful town. There was Beitman & Wolf's. And Martha's Millinery, her fly-specked window crowded with bonnets. Several old-timers in bib overalls lounged outside Lengel's Gun Shop.

Did the younger members of town still patronize the Red Onion Saloon? he wondered. He grinned at a sudden memory of the last ruckus he'd gotten into at the saloon, much to his grandma's dismay. She was always quoting Proverbs to him after an escapade at the Red Onion.

Those Bible verses he'd memorized at her knee were one of the things that got him through the horror of prison camp. He didn't really understand some of them very well, but they were somehow very comforting. Maybe when his life settled down a little, he could study the Scriptures for himself.

His smile faded. He knew the war had changed him and not for the better. Something inside him had turned hard and cold, and he realized that in reality he had little desire to study the Bible. After what he'd seen in the war, God didn't seem too likely. He pushed his grandmother's memory away and gazed out the window intently.

The train gave one final, wheezing bellow, then came to a shuddering stop under the overhang of the depot. Rand took a deep breath and stood up, pulling his haversack out from under his seat. His heart pounded as he limped toward the door. *Wouldn't it be grand if Pa or Jacob were in town? No chance of that, though,* he thought as he watched through the windows. For one thing, he was here a good week earlier than he'd written he'd be. Lot more likely to find them in the field on the way home, if Jacob were even here. *And if he survived the war,* an inner voice whispered.

His weak leg, cramped by the long trip, gave out as he stepped down, and he fell into an elderly, stooped man's surprised face. "Why—I–I cain't believe it! Rand Campbell, is it really you?" Liam, who had run the train station for as long as Rand could remember, grabbed him by the shoulders and peered into his face.

His hair was even more grizzled than Rand remembered, but his breath stank of garlic like usual, and Rand suppressed a grin. Liam's wife believed in garlic's medicinal qualities, so most folks steered clear of her specialties at the church picnics. "It's me all right, Liam."

"Rand," the old man gasped again before enfolding him in a bear hug. "We heered you was dead, boy."

Rand hugged him back until his words penetrated, then drew back in shock. "What do you mean, dead? I wrote my folks and Sarah every few weeks. I've been in the hospital in Washington." No wonder he hadn't heard from his family, he thought.

Liam pulled a filthy handkerchief from his pocket and wiped his face shakily. The surprise was almost too much for him. "Wait till Myra hears 'bout this!" He put the dirty cloth back in his pocket. "Don't know nothin' 'bout no letters. No one here got no letters, I'm sure. Yer folks been grievin' themselves to death over you. Had a memorial service at church for you last spring, and I ain't never seed so many people at one of them things." He stared in Rand's puzzled face. "I'm tellin' ya, we all thought you was dead, boy!"

Rand felt like he'd been punched in the stomach; he couldn't catch his breath. How could something like this have happened? "I–I sent a letter with Ben Croftner to give to Sarah," he stammered. "Didn't he make it back here?"

A look of surprise and something else Rand couldn't identify flickered across Liam's face. "Yeah, he got back—let's see.

Must be pert near six months ago." He paused and glanced quickly at Rand's face before continuing. "But he didn't say nothin' 'bout no letter."

Rand stared at him, a puzzled frown creasing his broad forehead. There was something odd in Liam's manner. "What aren't you telling me?" he asked, his keen brown eyes fixed on the old porter's face.

The man flushed. "Well, now—I–I guess you have to hear it sooner or later," he stammered. "Ben's s'posed to marry Sarah tomorrow. Right after church. Whole town's been invited. Ben's been struttin' 'round all important like."

The strength left Rand's knees, and he sat down on the passenger bench outside the depot. The implications of what Liam said began to sink in, along with a bitter anger at Ben's betrayal. And Sarah's. "He let her go on thinkin' I was dead," he said slowly. He stood up angrily and slung his haversack over one broad shoulder. "He let my family go on grieving and suffering. He'll pay for this," he spat through clenched teeth. Abruptly he turned south and strode off without saying good-bye to Liam, his slight limp more pronounced because of his fatigue and agitation.

The old man stared after him, a grin on his weathered face. "Sure would like to see Rand light into that Ben. He's been no-account since he was knee-high to a grasshopper," he muttered as he turned to go back into the depot. " 'Bout time he got his comeuppance."

Rand clamped down on the rage that was building in him. How could Ben do such a thing? And Sarah. How could she be so fickle? Why, he must have been declared dead only a few months before she took up with Croftner! Was that all the time she mourned someone she was supposed to love? His emotions felt raw, and he just couldn't seem to make any sense out of it.

By the time he made his way to the livery stable, paid for a horse, and swung up into the saddle, he was shaking with fury. He dug his heels into the mare's flank and set off toward home.

Being astride a horse again for the first time in a year cleared his thoughts, and he was more in control of his emotions by the time he pulled the mare off the road and headed up the deeply rutted track that followed the river. The fields were tawny with drying corn. Harvest would be in a few weeks. His heart quickened as the white two-story home on the hill overlooking the river came into view. Home! How he'd longed for this moment.

He pulled the horse up sharply, undecided. Should he go home first or go see Sarah and demand an explanation? He could just see the roof of the large Montgomery house over the next rise, and he let the horse prance on the path for a moment as he decided what to do.

No, he thought grimly as he dug his heels into the gelding's flank and turned up the Campbell lane. *My family first—at least they've mourned for me.*

By the time he reached the front yard, his heart was pounding and his palms were slick with sweat. A nagging headache persisted just behind his eyes. He pulled his horse to a stop and dismounted, a little disappointed no one was outside. As he approached the back door that led to the kitchen, through the window he could see his mother washing dishes. A wave of love welled up in him as he saw the new gray in her hair and the fine web of wrinkles at her eyes. He breathed in the familiar scent of apple pie baking in the oven.

His mother's back was to the door, and he watched her a moment as she picked up a dish and proceeded to wash it. "I think I heard a horse," she said to the little brown dog lying on the rug by her feet. "Probably one of the menfolk home." The little dog pricked up her ears and whined as she looked toward the door. His mother dipped the soapy plate in the pan of rinse water and laid it to drain on the wooden chopping block beside her.

Rand let the screen door bang behind him, but she didn't turn. "Don't bang the door," she said automatically just as Jody yipped and launched herself in a frenzy toward the door. She wiped her soapy hands on her apron and started to turn to see why the dog was so excited.

"Ma." Rand knelt and picked up the little dog as he stared at his mother.

She froze and Rand saw one emotion after another chase across her face. Uncertainty, disbelief, hope. She clutched her hands in the folds of her apron and swung slowly around to face him.

"Ma, I'm home." Rand patted Jody and laughed as the dog wriggled in his arms and licked his face joyously.

Her mouth gaping, Margaret stared at the figure standing in the sunlit area by the door.

"It's me, Ma. It's really me. I'm not dead."

Her own Rand, recognizable in spite of his gauntness, stood in front of the screen door, his brown eyes soft with love, the golden September sun shining on his handsome, square-jawed face, his deep dimples coming and going as his face worked with emotion. For just an instant, she thought it was a vision or an angel. Then she saw the deep lines of pain beside his mouth and the way his blue uniform hung on his thin frame and his ragged haircut. All these imperfections convinced her this was really her boy.

"Rand?" she croaked as she took a faltering step toward him. "Rand!" With a noise something between a cry and a croak, she threw herself into his arms as the tears started down her cheeks. After several moments, she drew away. "I can't believe it! Let me look at you." She held him at arm's length, then hugged him, laughing and crying as Jody licked both their faces and whined and wriggled in ecstasy.

Rand clutched his mother so tightly he was afraid he hurt her. For over a year, ever since he was captured, he'd longed for his ma's gentle touch on his brow. At night when he awoke bathed in sweat from the pain, he had ached to lay his head on her breast and hear her soothing voice as she sang to him. He had been so hurt and bewildered at her silence after his release. Every time the door to the hospital ward opened, he had expected to see her anxious face.

They both finally calmed down enough to sit at the kitchen table so he could explain what had happened. Margaret kept touching him to convince herself he was real while he talked and talked. He was on his third cup of coffee when they heard several horses cantering into the yard.

❦

Jacob looked in puzzlement at the strange horse tied to the hitching post. "You expectin' anyone?" he asked with a quizzical look at Shane and his pa.

Jeremiah shook his large head. "Looks like that new bay from Larson's livery. Must be someone from out of town."

They tied their horses to the post and headed toward the kitchen door. A low murmur of voices drifted out the screen door, and Jacob paused. *That almost sounds like Rand,* he thought, pain stabbing him. He didn't think he'd ever get over his older brother's death. There were even times when he thought he caught a glimpse of Rand in his favorite red plaid flannel shirt stride past just out of the corner of his eye. He shook off the memory and pushed into the kitchen as a dark-haired man, dressed in a blue Union uniform, rose unsteadily from the kitchen table and turned to face him.

"Jake."

Rand had coined his nickname, and no one said it quite the way he did. Jacob opened his mouth to question this smiling, dark-eyed stranger who looked like—but of course couldn't be—he was too thin. But the smile! And the look in those brown eyes, and those dimples!

"Rand!" Shane shrieked his brother's name and flung himself into Rand's waiting arms. A moment later all four men were hugging and slapping one another on the back, unashamed of the tears streaming from their eyes.

"It's really you, it's really you," Jacob said over and over as he stared at his brother as if memorizing his features.

"The good Lord answered our prayers after all." With a shaking hand, Jeremiah wiped at his eyes with his bandanna. He was breathing hard, as if he'd just run all the way from the back pasture to the house.

They sat down around the kitchen table as Margaret hurriedly poured them each a cup of coffee and joined them. Just as she sat down, they heard the front door slam.

Hannah, the eldest and only girl, hurried into the kitchen. "Sorry I'm late, Ma," she panted. She stopped short and looked at the group clustered around the table. Why was everyone crying, and smiling, too? Her puzzled stare stopped when her eyes met Rand's. She opened and closed her mouth several times, but no sound escaped.

"What! My gabby sister with nothing to say?" Rand stood, a teasing light in his eyes.

Hannah screamed and dropped the basket she was holding. Potatoes rolled across the wooden floor and she almost tripped on them as she rushed toward her brother. She threw herself into Rand's arms, and he picked her up and swung her around, kissing her soundly before setting her on her feet again.

"Let me look at you!" She held him at arm's length and frowned as she saw his thinness. "What's happened to you? We thought you were dead!"

She hung onto his arm as he limped back to the table and sat down. "I was just about to explain when you so rudely interrupted," he said with a grin. "Of course, that's nothing new—you've never learned how to be quiet."

"Very funny!" She punched him on the arm and sat down beside him.

"Ouch." He rubbed his arm, then grinned at his family. "Now, as I was about to say, I was captured outside Atlanta in

August of '64. I'd been on reconnaissance trying to see where the heaviest troops were. That's how I spent most of the war, slipping back and forth through enemy lines. The Rebs took me to Andersonville prison camp—"

"Andersonville!" Jacob interrupted, his voice filled with horror. "That camp is notorious. I heard the Union army found 12,000 graves there when the war was over."

Rand nodded. "I was lucky I wasn't one of them. You can't imagine how bad it was. We had to build our own shelters, usually just a lean-to made with whatever we could find. Blankets, clothing, sticks. Some of the men could only dig a hole in the ground and cover up with a single thin blanket. There were so many of us we just barely had enough space to lie down. And the food—"

He broke off and took a deep breath. "Well, it wasn't like yours, Ma. We were lucky if they gave us a little salt, maybe a half a cup of beans, and about a cup of unsifted cornmeal. A lot of men died from the inflamed bowels the stuff caused. One day I helped bury over a hundred bodies in a common grave." His face was white with the horror of the memories.

Margaret laid a trembling hand on his arm. "I just thank God you survived it, Son."

He covered her hand with his and smiled before continuing. "I was delirious by the time we were freed, a combination of dysentery and malnutrition." He smiled grimly. "The doctors tell me I weighed less than a hundred pounds when I was brought to the hospital. A skeleton really. I've spent the last six months at Harewood Hospital in Washington recuperating."

"Why didn't you write?" Hannah burst out.

"I wrote several times. At least once a month."

"We never received a single letter. Just a notification from the army of your death about the same time you say you were captured." Jacob's look was puzzled.

"I knew you weren't dead. I just knew it," Shane put in excitedly. "I told Sarah just last week!"

At the mention of Sarah's name, Rand looked at Jacob, his eyes no longer smiling. "What about Sarah, Jacob?"

Jacob started, then forced himself to look in his brother's hurt eyes.

"I already know she's going to marry Ben Croftner. How could she do that—didn't she mourn me at all?" There was a bitter taste in his mouth as Rand spat the words out.

"Mourn you? You idiot!" Hannah interrupted, standing up and raking a hand through her mane of chestnut hair. "We all feared for her sanity! She refused to eat for days. Even now she hardly smiles. And you know what a perky, bubbly little thing she has always been."

"Then why is she marrying Ben?"

Hannah hesitated, her eyes searching her brother's face. "William is dying," she sighed as she sat back down beside her brother. She took his hand gently as his face whitened in shock. "Sarah doesn't know, but William and Wade have pushed her to marry Ben right away. And Ben has promised Wade that fifty acres of prairie he's always coveted as a marriage settlement, Rachel told me. Wade's taken advantage of Sarah's apathy since the news of your death to convince her she owes it to the family to do this."

"Wade's always thought of himself instead of his family," Rand said angrily. "But there's something else you don't know." He stood and paced over to the window at the front of the kitchen, then wheeled to face them. "Ben has known all along I wasn't dead."

"What!" Margaret stood in agitation. "Are you sure?"

He nodded grimly. "Ben was with the troops who liberated the prison. I even gave him a letter to give to Sarah."

"Maybe he thought you died after he left," Margaret offered.

Jacob shook his head thoughtfully. "He knew we read it in the paper last fall. And that we received an official notification shortly after that. I'm positive he never gave Sarah any letter."

"What about all the letters I wrote from the hospital?" Rand sat down and stretched his aching leg out in front of him, rubbing it absently as he tried to figure out how Ben had pulled his little drama off.

"The mail service has been wretched," Jeremiah said. "Maybe they were lost."

"All of them?" Rand shook his head. "Not likely. Ben must have gotten hold of them somehow."

"Labe works in the post office," Shane said in a small voice. "But he's really nice. He wouldn't do anything like that."

His announcement silenced everyone. Finally Hannah spoke up in a soft, hesitant voice. "Surely Labe wouldn't tamper with the mail." But her tone indicated her own doubt.

"What other explanation is there, Sis?" Jacob jumped up angrily, his fists clenched.

Rand got purposely to his feet. "I'm going to see Sarah," he announced. "Then I'm going to get to the bottom of this."

Margaret held out a placating hand. "Let it go for now, Son. Try to get a handle on your anger before you talk to Ben."

Rand shook off her hand. "Let it go! After all I've been through, you want me to let it go? Ben needs to find out he can't treat a Campbell like that."

Margaret touched her son's cheek gently. "The war has changed you, Rand." She paused, searching for the right words. "You seem so harsh and headstrong. You've always been the even-tempered, rational one in the family."

Rand raked a weary hand through his thick hair. "What do you expect, Ma? For me to just forget how Ben lied and deceived the people I love? Well, I just can't do it. Maybe if I hadn't been through so much the last few years, I could. But I thought Ben was my friend. I trusted him. I think I deserve an explanation for what he's done."

Margaret bit her lip and her hand fell away from his arm. " 'Vengeance is mine, sayeth the Lord,' " she quoted softly.

Rand looked at her for a long moment, then grabbed his hat and strode toward the back door. Her words made him feel guilty and uneasy somehow, but he pushed the feelings away.

"Don't go see Ben without me," Jacob called to his retreating back, his voice tight with anger.

Rand nodded without looking back. He strode into the barn and grinned at the welcoming nicker. At least Ranger didn't think he was dead. He patted the horse's white nose lovingly, then saddled him and headed first toward the Montgomery farm. Then he'd settle with Ben Croftner.

four

Sarah took a sip of tea and tried to drag her attention back to Myra's conversation, but her thoughts kept whirling around. Tomorrow she would be Mrs. Ben Croftner. She thought she knew just how Joan of Arc must have felt the night before she was burned at the stake, and her spirit recoiled at the thought of what tomorrow would bring. The last few days had swept by in a daze and now her future was hurtling toward her at breathtaking speed. The light-hearted chatter of her friends around her, the brightly patterned quilt still attached to the quilting frame, the gifts heaped beside her, all served to deepen her sense of impending doom. She didn't want to leave her home, her comfortable, predictable life. And how well did she really know Ben? What if her new life was so different she couldn't adjust?

Suddenly aware of a strange hush in the room, Sarah looked around at the other ladies. They all wore the same look of shock and disbelief. Sarah twisted around to face the door herself, almost afraid to see what could cause such consternation among her friends.

She blinked at the figure blocking the sunlight as his broad shoulders spanned the doorway. Her eyes traveled up the gaunt frame to the face staring back at her intently. She gasped and began to rise to her feet. Was she dreaming? She put a hand to her throat.

"Sarah."

The voice was so familiar, so beloved. She gasped, then took a step toward him and reached out a trembling hand.

Rand caught her hand as she reached toward him. "Hello, Sarah."

"Rand?" Sarah could barely choke out the name. Was he

real? "Rand, is it really you?" Hesitantly she touched his square jawline and felt the rough stubble on his chin. "It is you!" She buried her face against his chest and burst into tears. *If it's a dream, I don't ever want to wake up,* she thought. But this was no dream. The rough texture of his uniform under her cheek, the familiar spicy tang of his hair tonic, and most importantly, the touch of his hands on her waist were all too vivid and real for it to be a dream.

Rebecca Stevens, the pastor's wife, motioned for the rest of the ladies to follow her into the kitchen. She closed the door behind them, her blue eyes dancing with joy and relief.

As soon as the door shut behind them, Rand pulled her away from his chest and she stared up into his brown eyes. "Where have you been? We thought you were dead!" she whispered, blinking back the tears. "You're so thin!"

"I know you were told I was dead. I stopped home first and Jacob told me." He explained all the events of the past year while Sarah's green eyes absorbed every detail of his appearance. He was too thin, but he looked grand in his blue uniform with the brass buttons gleaming and the cap perched on his dark hair.

"Why didn't you write?" she said when he paused for breath.

"I did."

She suddenly realized that he hadn't really embraced her yet. And there was a hidden something in his eyes. Was it pain? Anger? "What is it?" she asked, her throat tight. "What's wrong?"

He picked up her left hand; the diamond engagement ring Ben had given her only days before sparkled in the afternoon sun streaming through the lace curtains. "Why didn't you wait for me like you promised?" He dropped her hand and took a step back. "How could you do it, Sarah? I trusted you. The thought of you waiting here—loving me, I thought—was the only thing that kept me alive during those long months at Andersonville. The only thing that kept me sane."

"But, Rand—"

He interrupted her with a fierce look, his anger beginning to override the initial joy of their reunion. "Some of the other men got thrown over, but I never worried about that. Not my Sarah, I thought. She would be true no matter what happens. Sometimes I questioned why I was allowed to live when I saw all my friends die, but I knew it was because you were waiting on me. Depending on me to come back to you. Did our love mean so little to you?"

What was he saying? She began to sob again, only now the tears were of sorrow not joy. "We—we thought you were dead," she whispered. "Don't you understand?"

"All I understand is that you forgot me in only a few short months. And your wonderful new fiancé knew all along I wasn't dead."

"No, Rand, he told me—"

He seized her trembling shoulders, his face white with rage. "He knew, I tell you! I gave him a letter to give to you. Did you get a letter?"

"No, but there must be some mistake. Ben cried when he told me about how he found your body—"

"Yeah, I'm really dead, aren't I?"

"Bu—but Ben *saw* your body." She felt idiotic repeating herself, but her mind felt somehow sluggish and stupid. She couldn't seem to reconcile the two totally different stories.

"I tell you he knew all along I wasn't dead! He was with the troops who rescued me!"

"But we saw in the paper—"

"It was wrong and he knew it was wrong. And how do you explain the letter he neglected to give you?"

She suddenly understood he was accusing Ben of deliberately keeping the truth from her. "There must be some explanation. Ben wouldn't do something like that," she insisted stubbornly.

"And I've written you and my folks many times while I

was recuperating in Washington. You didn't get any of those letters, either. And you know why? Labe works at the post office!" He took off his hat and raked a hand through his thick hair. "How can you even stand there and defend what Ben's done?"

Her green eyes grew huge in her white face as she suddenly grasped the enormity of Ben's treachery. What a fool she'd been! How gullible she was! All that phony sympathy—and the details he'd offered to prove to her Rand was really dead! "But we didn't know! How can you blame me for it?"

Rand took a deep breath and she flinched from the pain and anger she saw burning in his brown eyes. "I reckon what really hurts the most is just how quick you took up with Croftner. I didn't realize until now how little you loved me. And that hurts, Sarah. That really hurts." He wheeled to the door and wrenching it open, stalked out.

"Rand!" she cried after his retreating figure. "Don't go. I do love you!" She ran after him, but he ignored her pleading voice and stomped down the porch steps. "Wait. Please, wait." She caught his arm, but he shrugged it off and swung up onto Ranger's back.

He gazed down at her white face, the muscles in his throat working. "Maybe we can talk again in a few days. I just can't right now." He took a deep breath, then his jaw hardened as he stared down at her for one long moment. He shook his head slightly as though to clear it, then dug his heels into the gelding's flank and turned down the lane.

She stared after him in horror and disbelief. He had to listen to her—he just had to! She sank down on the porch step and buried her face in her hands. The diamond ring Ben had given her just last week was a little too big and it scratched her cheek where it had twisted toward her palm. She pulled her hand away and stared at the ring in rage and revulsion. Wrenching it off her finger and standing up, she threw it as hard as she could toward the woods to her left. She could see it winking in the sunlight as it arced up then disappeared into the burnished canopy of leaves. She couldn't stand to have it touch her or to even see it. It was just a reminder of her gullibility.

The buckboards and buggies were gone, and the house was quiet when she walked listlessly back inside. The ladies had all discreetly gone home, but the clutter left from the quilting bee was still strewn about the parlor. Rachel had left to go pick up Wade in town. She kicked aside a pincushion and sat down. She felt numb, drained. There had to be some way to make Rand see, but she was just too tired to find it right now. *But at least he's alive,* she thought. What a wonderful miracle! She curled up on the sofa, her knees drawn up to her chest. She was so very tired— When she woke up she'd think of some way to get through to Rand.

five

Rand paused for a moment on a knoll overlooking the Campbell home sprawling below him. *This is some homecoming,* he thought with a bitter twist to his lips. He had so many conflicting emotions. His love for Sarah told him to forgive her and understand the situation, but his overwhelming disappointment just wouldn't let him. Everything was so different than he'd expected. *I always thought her love was the kind that only comes once in a lifetime,* he thought. And to find out now that she'd promised to marry Ben while he lay near death was just too much to take in.

He urged Ranger down the lane toward the house. He had to see Ben. Right now. His wounded pride demanded a face-to-face explanation from Ben for his treachery. But he'd promised Jacob not to go without him, so he would wait long enough to keep his promise. He'd always prided himself on the value of his word, unlike a certain woman he knew, he thought with pain twisting his lips.

He was reasonably certain where Ben could be found, too. Unless he'd changed a lot in the past two years, he'd be at the back table at the Red Onion. Ben was certainly going to be surprised when he walked in. Or maybe not. Maybe he had read his letters before he destroyed them.

The family was sitting around the kitchen table when he stepped in the back door. Pa was saying grace, so Rand stood silently, his head bowed. As soon as he heard the amen, he limped to the table and dropped into the empty chair beside Jacob.

Margaret had peeked during the prayer when she heard the screen door open and breathed a sigh of relief when she saw

Rand come in. He really was there. She wanted to drink in the sight of him, even though his face was set in grim lines with no trace of the half-smile he usually wore even in sleep. She smiled at him when he sat down, but even then, his face remained set and strained.

"You still want to go with me, Jacob?"

Jacob looked up at his brother's grim face and his own darkened. "I'll get my hat."

Margaret saw he was still not ready to listen to reason, but she had to try. "Wait till tomorrow, Son. Think it over with a clear head."

"Think about it! That's all I've done for the past three hours. Ben is going to have to explain what he's done." His voice shook with emotion, then rose. "I can't even enjoy being home until I see him. I can't just pick up my life where I left off as if none of this has happened." He stood abruptly as Jacob came back into the kitchen.

The two young men mounted up and rode out silently, the stillness broken only by the clopping of the horses' hooves and the croaking of the frogs along the riverbank. The fecund smell from the river wafted in on the breeze. Jacob kept stealing glances at the outline of Rand's set jaw, illuminated occasionally by the last shafts of sunlight through the thick curtain of leaves above their heads. He wasn't sure he recognized his brother in this jaw-clenched man beside him.

"You know where Ben lives?"

"He bought that fancy brick house on Main Street. You know the one Judge Jackson built?"

Rand looked at him in surprise. "How'd he ever afford a place like that?"

"Land speculation, mostly. And investments after the war, I guess. He's pretty closemouthed about it."

Rand followed his brother as they cantered up the steep Wabash Street hill and turned down Main Street, dimly illuminated by gaslights. His anger against Ben deepened at this new revelation. *God never promised life would be fair,* he could almost hear his grandma whisper. He shook his head to clear the thought out and clenched his jaw tighter.

‰

When Sarah awoke, the situation seemed even more dreadful to her. The hardest thing to accept was her own naiveté. She surely hadn't shown much of the clear-headed thinking she'd always prided herself on, she thought wryly. And the realization of how easily she'd been deceived really stung. The clock chimed, reminding her how late it was, so she hurriedly threw more wood into the cookstove and sat down at the table to peel potatoes. Papa would be back from town any time, and Wade, demanding supper, wouldn't be far behind with Rachel. There was a heavy cloud cover, and the smell of rain came through the open window. It was already dark although it was barely six o'clock.

"Sarah."

She jumped at the sudden sound. She had been so lost in thought she hadn't heard the knock on the door. She turned and whitened when she saw Ben. She clenched her fists, then rose and took a step toward him. "How dare you come here after what you've done! How could you do such a thing to me—to Rand's family?"

"Rand, always Rand! Don't you care about my feelings at all?" Tears of self-pity welled up in his eyes, then he suddenly noticed her bare left hand. "Where's your ring?" he demanded hoarsely, grasping her shoulders in a painful grip.

Sarah stared at him, her green eyes enormous. "You can't possibly think I would marry you after all you've done?" She twisted vainly in his painful grip. "After you lied and tricked me? You're not the man I thought you were at all. I could never marry someone I couldn't trust."

Ben ignored her retort. "Where—is—your—ring?" He punctuated every word with a shake, and her hair tumbled out of the pins and down her back.

"I threw it into the woods," she said with a defiant toss of her head.

His fingers bit deeper into the soft flesh of her arms, and she winced. "Do you have any idea how much that ring cost?" he shouted.

"Is money all you care about? Don't you care about the pain you've caused?" She couldn't believe how quickly his tender, well-mannered facade crumbled.

He saw her appalled expression, and his own face hardened. He seized her elbow and yanked her toward the door.

"What are you doing?" Panicked, Sarah tried to free herself. "Let go of me!" She heard the fabric rip under her elbow as she tried to wrench her arm out of his grip.

"You're mine, Sarah, and no one else's. You're coming with me, and Campbell will never find us." He hauled her struggling form through the door and hoisted her up beside Labe, waiting in the buckboard, the brim of his hat pulled low to shield his face from the misty rain just beginning to fall.

Labe's face was pale, and his mouth worked soundlessly. "I'm sorry, Sarah," he finally whispered as he tied her hands together with a piece of rough rope. "I tried to talk him out of this, but there was no stoppin' him."

"Shut up," his brother snarled as he crawled up beside Sarah. "Everything arranged?"

Labe nodded uncertainly. "Bedrolls are in the back, 'long with everthin' else you said."

He's insane, Sarah thought when she saw the strange glint in his eyes. With renewed fear, she lunged backward, intending to crawl over the bedrolls and out the back, but Ben was too quick for her. He sat her back in the seat with a bone-jarring thump. "If you don't sit still, I'll truss you up like a chicken," he warned.

And he would, too. She could see it in his eyes. Shivering from the cold needles of rain that pelted down in earnest now, she huddled in the seat and tried to think of how to get out of this mess.

Ben picked up the reins, but before he could slap them against the horse's flank, two riders came around the curve of the lane. He squinted in the near darkness, his eyes widening as he recognized Rand and Jacob.

"Rand!" Sarah cried in relief. She started to clamber over Labe, but Ben grabbed her arm.

"Let go of her, Ben. This is between you and me." Rain dripping from the broad brim of his army hat, Rand slid to the ground and walked toward the buckboard, skirting the widening mud puddles. Jacob followed close behind, his fists clenched.

The click as Ben drew back on the trigger of his pistol was muffled in the pattering rain. "Don't come any closer, Campbell."

Rand stopped. "Why'd you do it, Ben? Why did you lie to everyone?"

All the pent-up rage and hatred burst out of Ben like a torrent of pus from a festering wound. "It was always you! Even my pa thought the sun rose and set with you. Ever since you stopped and helped him mend our fence and round up all the escaped cattle. It was always, 'Ben, why don't you study as hard as Rand,' or 'Ben, I hope you turn out as well as that oldest Campbell boy.' I got so sick of being compared to you. I don't know why he expected so much of me anyway. He was just a no-account drunk all his life."

His face whitened as he aimed the gun at Rand. "And then there was Sarah. You never noticed how she mooned over you for years. Instead you chased after that Baxter girl, and I hoped Sarah would come to care for me once you were out of the picture. But no. You had to finally set your sights on my girl."

"I was never your girl!" Sarah leaned toward him slightly, her eyes on the gun.

Ben continued as if he didn't hear her. "But when I got

back from the war five months ago and found out they all thought you were dead, I thought fate was finally smiling on me, and Sarah would finally be mine. But you had to come back early and spoil everything, just like you always have. But you're not going to ruin things for me ever again." He brought the pistol up higher with sudden determination and fired.

Just as he pulled the trigger, Sarah leaned against him with all her might, and the shot went wild. "Run, Rand!" she screamed.

But instead of running, Rand launched himself at Ben and dragged him down off the buckboard seat. The two men thrashed in the muck. Rand gave into the rage and threw a hard right swing that connected solidly with Ben's cheek. Ben reeled back and hit his head on the wheel of the buckboard as he fell. Rand stared down at the other man lying on the ground.

He pushed his hair out of his eyes, and with an unsteady hand he stepped away from Ben. Was he dead? He stared at Ben's pale face, relieved to see him draw a ragged breath. He felt shaken at how easily he could have killed someone who was once a friend. *Ma was right,* he thought. *I have changed.*

Shivering and soaked to the skin, Sarah climbed awkwardly out of the buckboard on rubbery legs and almost fell. "Thank God, you're all right!"

He untied the ropes on her hands gently, then stepped away. "What were you doing with Ben, Sarah?"

She stared at him in dismay. Surely he didn't think she was running off with Ben willingly? Her green eyes flashed, and she raised her chin defiantly. "I was eloping, of course. Wasn't it obvious?" She expected him to laugh, but instead he drew back from her. She caught his arm again. "Rand, surely you don't believe—" She bit her lip as he turned away, his eyes hooded.

Jacob touched his brother's arm as Ben drew a groaning breath. "Rand, I think one of us had better ride after Doc Seth.

Ben doesn't look too good."

"I'll go." Rand shook off Sarah's restraining hand and mounted his horse.

She stood looking after him in dismay. He had to listen to her eventually. He just had to!

six

Rand could sense Sarah's gaze as she stood beside Doc Seth, but he resisted looking at her. The rain had soaked through every scrap of his clothing and he shivered as a buggy came sloshing around the corner and a slight, frail figure painfully clambered down.

"William."

Sarah's father turned at the familiar, deep voice as Rand stepped out from the shadows. Tears started to fill William's eyes as he opened his arms and drew Rand into an embrace. "My dear boy, I heard the news in town. What a happy day this is for all of us."

Rand was shocked when he saw William's condition, even though Hannah had warned him. William had always been frail, but vibrant in spite of it all. Where was the man he'd idolized all his life? He didn't recognize him in this stoop-shouldered man with deep lines of pain around his mouth. He felt tears flood his own eyes as he hugged William. The older man's frailty reminded him of a dying baby bird he'd found once, its bones thin and brittle. "It–it's good to see you, sir," he stammered, trying to hide his dismay.

"You, too, son. You, too." William drew back and wiped his eyes shakily with his handkerchief. "What's going on here?"

"I gather that Ben was trying to force Sarah to go off with him," Rand said, and then went on to explain Ben's deception.

"I can't believe it," William said, shaking his head. "I really liked that boy. He seemed so ambitious and honest. I really admired the way he pulled himself up out of his family circumstances. Wade will be very upset."

Doc Seth straightened up and stepped over to Rand and

William. "He'll be all right. But he's sure going to wake up with a sore head tomorrow. I told Labe to take him home and put him to bed, and I'll look in on him tomorrow." He thrust out a hand to Rand. "Good to have you home, young Campbell. Amelia told me the news."

Rand shook his hand. "Tell her I'll stop by and see her soon."

He broke off, and they all turned as they heard another horse and buggy canter into the yard.

Wade slid down from his buggy, his jowled face florid with outrage. "What's going on here?" he demanded. He didn't bother to help his wife down, but stomped over to where his father stood. His wife had told him of Rand's return and his bad mood was evident.

Joel slid down from the buggy eagerly and bounded into Rand's arms exuberantly. "Rand! Oh, Rand!"

Rand laughed and hugged him tightly. He loved Sarah's little brother as much as his own. "How you doing, Half-Pint?"

"Great. I've missed you so much. When can we go fishing?"

Rand grinned at the familiar question. He'd always felt sorry for the lad. William's health prevented much of the usual father-son relationship, and Wade was too self-centered to take any of his precious time for such mundane things as fishing. "Soon," he said.

He pulled a hand free and thrust it out as Wade stomped up. "Good to see you, Wade." It wasn't really, but he could at least make an attempt at civility, he thought.

Wade ignored the outstretched hand. "I thought we were rid of you for good! I want you off my land, Campbell. Now!"

Rand lowered his hand and put it back in his pocket. "I was kind of hoping you'd changed, Wade. I should have known better."

Wade took a step toward Rand, his face reddening. "You—"

"That's enough!" William's voice boomed out in a sudden

surge of strength. "Your treatment of a guest in our home is unacceptable, Wade. And as long as I own this property, no friend will be turned away—least of all Rand. You have no idea of the wrong that's been done to him over the past few months."

Wade glared at his father, his massive hands clenched. "Who cares? I was just glad to be rid of him. I don't want him showing up now to spoil all our plans."

"What you want doesn't matter to me. And you know as well as I do that Sarah would never marry Ben now, anyway."

Wade's color deepened. "How do you know her feelings haven't changed? Ben would make a much better husband than Campbell."

"It depends on your definition of a good husband. Money isn't everything. I wouldn't want my daughter to marry someone who could deceive her the way Ben has." William directed a slight smile Sarah's way. "Ask your sister if she would marry him now that Rand is back."

Sarah shook her head. "You know I wouldn't."

The muscles in Wade's face worked as he clenched his jaw. "But what about the land?" He was eager to take possession of the thirty acres of rich soil in the prairie Ben had promised to give him if Sarah agreed to marry him.

"Is that all you care about? More land, more money?" William shook his head wearily. "I'm telling you right now, if you do anything to hurt Sarah or Rand, you won't have *this* land or house."

Wade stared at his father. "You'd cut me out of your will?"

"In a minute. Now get in the house until you can get a civil tongue in your head."

Wade glanced angrily at Sarah, then swung his massive head toward Rand before stomping into the house. He let the screen door slam shut behind him. Rachel sighed and followed him.

"Good for you, Papa." Sarah slipped her small hand into his. "Wade's had it coming for too long. I should never have let him get away with his arrogance for so long." William took his hat off and rubbed his forehead wearily. The confrontation had drained him. "Come in out of the rain, Sweetheart. You and Rand can have the parlor. I'm just going to have a bite to eat and go to bed." He shook Rand's hand. "Stop by tomorrow, and we'll talk. I'm just as eager as Joel to hear the full story." He walked into the house, his shoulders stooped.

But an order from his father wouldn't stop Wade for long, Sarah thought as she watched him stumble up the steps and into the house. Why did Wade hate Rand so? She shook her head in puzzlement. Ever since she could remember there had been an unspoken antagonism between the two men. And Rand had tried. But every overture he'd made had been ignored or ridiculed.

She pushed the disturbing puzzle out of her mind and turned back to Rand. "Rand, can we talk?"

"There's nothing to say right now." His tone was abrupt. "I still don't know how I feel about you or anything else." He took off his sopping hat and ran a weary hand through his wet hair. "And Wade has a point. Maybe your feelings *have* changed."

"Campbell!" Ben's hoarse cry interrupted them.

Ben raised his head from the back of the buckboard and gave Rand a long look filled with hatred. "This isn't over, Campbell. You'll never have her. Never. You just remember that." His head fell back against the floor of the buckboard as Labe slapped the reins against the horse's flank, but he watched them until he was out of sight, a burning hatred in his eyes.

Sarah shivered. "I think he means it," she said. "Watch your back, Rand."

"I can take care of myself." He saw her shiver again. "You're soaked to the bone," he said. "I'll come back and talk in a few days. You go on in now. Just give me some time."

Sarah hesitated, her eyes searching his sober face. Time?

How much time? But she left the questions unanswered and walked wearily up the porch steps, her spirits as low as her wet skirt dragging in the mud. She turned to watch Rand and Jacob mount up and ride down the lane and around the curve. Didn't he realize how much time they'd wasted already?

She was shaking uncontrollably by the time she dragged herself up the steps and into her room. There had to be a way to get through to him, she thought, as she pulled off her dripping clothes and left them in a puddle in the middle of the floor. Her teeth chattering, she climbed into bed and pulled the down comforter up over her shaking shoulders. There just had to be.

❧

The next morning Rand woke disoriented. The familiar clanging of trays in the hallway and the squeak of nurses' shoes hurrying with breakfast trays was missing. Sunshine streamed in the window and illuminated suddenly familiar surroundings. The toy soldiers Grampa had carved for him when he was five were lined up on a battered chest against the wall. His fingers stroked the brightly colored quilt, soft and faded with numerous washings. The rug on the unpainted wooden floor was as threadbare as he remembered it. He glanced at the space next to him. Jacob was nowhere to be seen, but the familiar indentation on the pillow brought a lump to Rand's throat. How good it was to be home!

He jumped out of bed, suddenly eager to get downstairs. He wouldn't worry about anything today, he decided as he splashed cold water on his face. He was just going to enjoy being with his family again after three long years. No uniform either, he thought, opening his closet. He grabbed a pair of overalls and his favorite plaid shirt and pulled them on. The pants hung around his waist, and they were too short, but they would have to do.

By the time he pulled on socks and boots, the aroma of coffee and bacon filled the air and made his stomach rumble hungrily. The low murmur of voices quickened his steps as hurried down the stairs.

His mother spun around as he stepped into the kitchen. "I was just coming to wake you." Her eyes noticed the bagginess of his pants, and she frowned. "I fixed ham and eggs, grits, flapjacks, and coffee. I'll have you fattened up in no time." She stepped into his arms for a quick, reassuring hug.

Rand grinned as he squeezed her, breathing in the faint fragrance of roses that clung to her. She wouldn't be Ma without that scent. He remembered gathering wild roses every summer for her to make sachets for her bureau drawers. He dropped his arms as she bustled over to the cookstove and offered him a plate piled high with food. His mouth watered as he took it from her and sat down between Shane and Jacob.

Hannah came hurrying in as Rand took his first sip of strong, hot coffee. Her face brightened as she saw Rand shoveling another forkful of eggs into his mouth. "Now I am sure it's really you," she said as she slipped into the chair opposite him. "The brother I remember was always eating."

Rand, a wicked grin on his face, caught Jacob's eye and gave a meaningful nod. "How come you're still here, anyway, Sis?" he asked. "I thought you would have been successful in trapping a husband by now."

"Come on, Rand, be realistic." Jacob poked his older brother with an elbow. "Who would have her? She has always been the ugliest Campbell."

Rand stared at his sister thoughtfully. "Yeah, I forgot about that big nose of hers. And all that hair."

"Not to mention her temper! Her tongue could cut a man to ribbons." Jacob grinned at the rising color on Hannah's face.

Rand knew they'd get a reaction when they hit on her sore spot. She was always moaning about her nose. Personally, Rand didn't see anything wrong with it, but she seemed to think it didn't match the pert ones described in her favorite novels.

She flushed a deep red, then burst into tears.

"Hey, I'm sorry, Sis." Rand's voice was dismayed. He hadn't expected this much of a reaction. He slid over and put an arm around her. "You know we were only teasing. I've always liked your nose."

Hannah just cried harder. "It's not that," she finally sputtered as Rand handed her his bandanna. She drew a deep breath. "It's just so wonderful to have you here, to see Jacob smile again, to hear your voice—" She stopped and gulped.

The dimples deepened in Rand's cheeks as he stared at his sister. "It sure is good to be home," he burst out. "To be with you all again just like before this crazy war ever happened. You don't know how afraid I was to get home. I was so scared when no one answered my letters."

Jeremiah and Margaret had been watching the exchange between their children with indulgent smiles, and Margaret's eyes welled with tears at Rand's words. She dabbed at her eyes with a lace-edged hanky, too overcome to talk.

Jeremiah forced back tears in his own eyes, then cleared his throat gruffly. "You're just in time to help with the farming, too," he said heartily. "It's almost more than Shane and I can handle. I've tried to talk your brother into staying home, but he won't listen. Now I'll have some help come spring."

Rand glanced at Jacob apprehensively. Hadn't Jacob told them of his plans? He and his brother had laid awake for hours talking last night. He'd been hoping that by now Jacob would have broken the news to their father. His brother shook his head slightly.

Jeremiah saw the wordless exchange. "What is it?" he asked, his eyes traveling from one to the other.

Rand hated to disappoint his pa. "I—I won't be able to stay long, Pa," he stammered. "I'm in the Third Cavalry. I can stay for about a week, but then I have to report for duty." He winced at the stricken look in his mother's eyes. "I've been garrisoned at Fort Laramie."

"Not you, too!" Hannah stood twisting her hands in her apron. "The Indians have been rampaging for months out there. Isn't it bad enough we're losing Jacob?"

"That's why so many of us are being sent out there. And I've found out in the past couple of years how much I enjoy the cavalry. I've always wanted to see the frontier. Maybe I can find my own spread while I serve my country a few more years. Besides, it's what I want—I volunteered."

"You can't!" Jeremiah rose to his feet. "Why do you think I've worked so hard on this farm? Always expanding, always looking for ways to make more money?" He put an arm around his wife. "It's been for you! For you and your brothers. I agreed to let Jacob go against my better judgment, but you've always been the one who had a feel for the land. I forbid you to go!"

Rand saw his mother flinch as the words echoed in the warm kitchen. His face hard and unyielding, he stood and faced his father. "You forbid? You forget I'm a grown man, Pa."

Margaret laid a gentle hand on her son's arm. "Your pa is just concerned, Rand. Can't you think about staying home now and letting us all begin to heal? You can raise horses right here on land that's been in the Campbell family for twenty-five years instead of fighting Indians to gain a small piece of land in some God-forsaken wilderness. You haven't been with us for three years."

His mother had always been able to change his mind in the past, and he fought against the soft persuasion in her voice. "I can't, Ma." He raked a hand through his hair. "I've fought worse than Indians in the last three years. And I know what it's like to be hungry and alone. It's something I have to do. Maybe it's just because I need to prove something to myself, to build my own dreams with my own sweat, but I have to go."

Jeremiah took a long look at his son's granite face, then wheeled and stomped from the room. Margaret opened her mouth to try again, but one look at the firm set to Rand's mouth changed her mind. Her eyes filling with tears, she hurried from the kitchen.

Always the peacemaker, Hannah cleared her throat and laughed self-consciously. "Land sakes, who could forget the way you've always had with horses and cattle. When Ma was carryin' Jacob, she asked you if you wanted a baby brother or sister. You looked up with those brown eyes of yours all serious and said, 'If it's all the same to you, Ma, I'd just as soon have a horse.' "

Laughter diffused the tension as they heard the familiar story. Jacob punched Rand in the arm. "Yeah, and you've been treating me like a beast of burden ever since!"

When the laughter faded, Hannah looked at her brother and said softly, "You are taking Sarah, aren't you?"

Rand looked quickly at her expectant face. "No," he said finally. "Not right now. I need some time to accept all that's happened. I'll keep in touch, and down the road, we'll see if we can work things out." He folded his arms across his chest. "And anyway, that area is no place for a woman. She'd soon get sick of being confined to the fort. You know how independent she is."

"Jacob is taking Amelia. It must not be too dangerous."

He saw the mutinous expression on Hannah's face as she opened her mouth to argue further. "Don't push me, Sis. I know you're concerned, but I have to be sure in my own mind why she took up with Ben. She was mighty young when I left for the war—only sixteen. I need to be sure she knows her own mind."

Hannah sighed impatiently. "Why are men so thick-headed?" she asked, rolling her eyes in exasperation.

Rand grinned and pushed away from the table. "It's the only protection we have against you women." He stood up and stretched. "Better get to the fields. I'll help all I can while I'm here."

"What about your leg?" Hannah asked anxiously.

"I feel fine, Sis. And I need to work at getting my strength back." He pushed back his chair, grabbed his hat, and followed his brothers out the door.

❧

Sarah sighed as she stared across the river. What could she do to change Rand's mind? She hadn't heard a word from him all day. Should she just swallow her pride and go find him? But he'd said to give him some time. Tears welled up in her eyes as she leaned down and picked up a flat rock. She skimmed it across the water, and it skipped three times. *Not very good,* she told herself. *You're losing your touch.* She reached down for another rock.

"The last time I saw you do that, it skipped six times."

She turned immediately and a bright smile lit her face when she saw Rand. It was almost as if her hopeless wishing had conjured him up. "Oh, Rand, I'm so glad you came," she said as she scrabbled to her feet and hurried toward him. He held out his arms, and she rushed into them.

She buried her face in his broad chest and clung until he lifted her chin and kissed her. As his lips touched hers, she wrapped her arms around his neck and kissed him back with all the love in her heart. His passionate response convinced her she hadn't lost him after all.

"I tried to stay away, Green Eyes, but I couldn't," he whispered. He loosed his grip on her with an effort.

"I'm so sorry about Ben," she began.

"It's not your fault," he interrupted. "I realized it as soon as I cooled down enough to think. I can't blame you for wanting to go on with your life."

"You are my life. Nothing seemed real with you gone. I knew I couldn't be happy, so I thought if everyone else were happy, it would be enough. But I was already beginning to regret promising to marry him."

"Then you still want to marry me?"

She smiled. Didn't he know without asking? "More than

anything in the world." She stopped and looked up at him, her eyes sparkling with joy. "James Benson left on the wagon train last May and his cabin is still empty. We can live there until our place is built on our knoll."

Rand's smile faded and he looked away. "I can't stay, Sarah. I'm still in the cavalry. I'm heading out west in a couple of days."

Shock darkened her eyes. Not staying here? She stared at him as his words soaked in. "But we've always planned to build on the knoll and help Papa with the farm. He's not well, Rand. I can't go running off out west and leave him."

"Your pa will understand. He came here with your ma and settled just like I want to do. He wasn't content to stay in Philadelphia."

"That was different. He was poor and had no prospects. You have land here, both mine and yours from your pa. I can't believe your pa will let you do this. He was very upset about Jacob's plans to leave." Surely Rand wasn't serious about this scheme. They'd made too many other plans.

"It's not different. Your pa wanted to build something on his own just like I do. I don't want to take something another man built. There's so much opportunity out west, Sarah. Land for the taking, gold, new businesses. It will be a great life. Besides, do you really think Wade and I could get along well enough to work together?"

"I *can't* go," she said frantically. Couldn't he see that? "I couldn't leave Papa. You haven't seen how ill he's been. He seems to go downhill every day. It would kill him for me to leave."

"I know he would understand. Let's go ask him." He took her arm and started purposely toward the house, but she pulled away.

"No! I don't want to upset him. I just can't go now. Can't you wait a few years? Just until he doesn't need me?"

"*Now* is the time of opportunity, Sarah. Besides I have my

orders and a letter to deliver for General Sherman. I have to go."

Sarah took a deep breath and stepped back from him. "And I have to stay." Tears filled her eyes as she saw Rand's face harden. She *couldn't* leave Papa. Why couldn't he understand that? He just didn't seem to be the same man who'd left three years ago. He was harder, more unbending.

"That's your answer then? After all we've been through? After all your protests of how much you love me, that's your answer? You're not the woman I thought you were, Sarah. Not the woman at all." He turned and left her standing on the path.

She opened her mouth to call him back, but the words died in her throat. What was the use? She couldn't go and he wouldn't stay. It was as simple as that. He didn't really love her or he wouldn't ask her to leave Papa. Not as sick as Papa was. Couldn't Rand see that? She choked back the tears in her throat and rubbed at her dry eyes. Her life was in shambles, and there seemed to be no solution.

seven

The train shrieked and puffed out a billow of soot as Rand, Jake, and Shane climbed down from the buckboard. Leaving his mother and father had been rough. Ma had cried, then pressed his grandma's Bible into his hand before hurrying away, and Pa wouldn't even come out of the barn to say good-bye. Shane snuffled, and Rand ruffled his hair, then hugged him. "I'm counting on you to take care of the family, Squirt."

Shane bit his quivering lip and nodded, straightening his shoulders. He trotted around behind the buckboard, and heaving the saddle over one shoulder, led Ranger to the waiting train. Rand's horse would accompany him west.

Rand hefted the haversack over his right shoulder and picked up the hamper of food and his satchel. He hesitated, suddenly indecisive. Why not stay for a while longer? General Sherman had told him to take more time to get back on his feet if he needed to. The letter would wait a few days. Maybe he should go see Sarah just once more and see if things could be worked out.

"All aboard!"

The conductor's shout broke his mood, and Rand shook himself mentally. Of course, he was going. This was what he wanted. With one last look at his brothers, he raced toward the slowly moving train and jumped up the steep steps. He caught one last glimpse of Jacob, standing alone with one arm upraised, his arm around his younger brother. Rand waved until the buckboard with the two figures beside it was no longer in view, then took a deep breath and made his way to a vacant seat. His great adventure was about to begin.

He sat next to a man, obviously a pig farmer from the odor that hung about him, who talked incessantly. Rand would just be dozing off into a fitful sleep and the man would ask him a question. By the time the long, thirty-six-hour trip was over, his eyes were scratchy, his throat was sore, and his chest hurt from coughing the black soot the small potbellied stove belched out. His leg ached from being in the narrow, cramped seat, and he limped heavily as he made his way to the door and out into the fresh air.

Kansas City was a sprawling assortment of wooden shops and storefronts. The streets teemed with horses and cattle, buggies and buckboards. And people. Everywhere people hurried across the muddy streets and crowded the uneven boardwalks. Rand felt invigorated by the hustle and bustle, despite the smell of manure and the distant lowing of cattle from the stockyards. *Someday I'll bring my own cattle to Kansas City or a cow town like it,* he thought with a thrill.

Across from the depot was the Holladay stagecoach station, and he walked across the street and stood in line behind another soldier. "Heading to Fort Leavenworth, too?" he asked him.

The other man turned with a friendly grin on his open, friendly face. "Sure am. Been on leave and kinda hate to go back. You new?"

"Captain Rand Campbell." He thrust out a soot-streaked hand. "But I'll just be there a few months. Until the snows pass. Then on to Fort Laramie—at least I think so."

"If that don't beat all. So am I! Lieutenant Isaac Liddle." He shook Rand's proffered hand, and taking off his wide-brimmed hat, wiped his forehead with a bandanna. "What unit you with?"

"H Troop, Third Cavalry. You?"

"Third Battalion. You're going to like Old Bedlam. You heard of it?"

Rand shook his head, liking the looks of his companion.

Isaac reminded him in some way of Jacob. Auburn hair and a dusting of freckles but the same muscular build and quiet but friendly manner as Jacob. Strong, capable hands. A man you could depend on. And from what he'd heard of the Indian Wars, you wanted that kind of man around.

Isaac grinned. "It's what we call the single officers' quarters. It came by its name legitimate. A lot of loud shenanigans goes on at all hours. At least I assume that's where you'll be quartered. I don't see a pretty lady with you. You're not married?"

A shadow darkened Rand's eyes. "No," he said shortly, pushing away an image of Sarah's heart-shaped face and dancing green eyes.

"I was hopin'. Fort Laramie doesn't have many women right now." Isaac was a perceptive man, and he saw the animation drain from Rand's face. He put his hat back on and changed the subject. "Where you from?"

"Wabash, Indiana. Born and raised on a farm about two miles out of town." Rand was grateful for the change in topic. "Where you hail from?"

"El Paso, Texas." He held one hand out in front of him hastily when he saw Rand's eyebrows raise. "But I fought for the Union."

That explained his accent, Rand thought. The line moved forward, and they followed. "What brought you so far from home?" Rand asked.

"Always hankered to see the West for myself. Figured joining the army was going to be the only way to do it. I'm the youngest in a family of seven boys, so I knew I'd never have anything for myself back home. I've asked the good Lord to help me find a place to settle down and raise racehorses."

"I aim to have cattle and stock horses someday. But I like the army for now. It's a good way to see the frontier." Rand continued to become acquainted with his new companion as the line moved slowly forward, until finally they had their tickets. Rand only had to pay for his luggage since he was riding Ranger instead of traveling on the stage.

Isaac crowded in with eight other soldiers, with three more squeezed outside on top. When Rand saw the bouncing, lurching ride, he was thankful to be riding his bay gelding.

Every ten miles or so they stopped at a way station for a break. Each one was the same. A small adobe building, a hut really, where they drew water to wash away a little of the dust and bolted down a nearly inedible meal of beans and hard, moldy bread. He was glad to see the small encampment of Fort Leavenworth by the day's end.

૨ล

Rand had been at Fort Leavenworth only two weeks when he and Isaac were unexpectedly ordered to proceed on to Fort Kearny and then to Fort Laramie. The weather had been unseasonably balmy, and the army wanted some reinforcements at Fort Laramie as soon as possible. He was a little sorry to leave the jolly little community behind, but he couldn't still a thrill of excitement as he fell into place behind the long column of men and supplies plodding toward the west.

By the time they arrived at Fort Laramie, Rand felt like he'd known his comrades all his life. He settled into Old Bedlam happily. The officers were a congenial group who loved a good time. Most evenings they gathered in the game room for cards or checkers. His days were full and his duties varied. He was sure he had made the right decision.

He'd been at Fort Laramie a week when he was ordered to lead a detachment to meet a column from Fort Kearny. Major DuBois and his retinue were expected to be in the column, so Rand wore his dress uniform. His brass buttons and buckles glimmered in the sunshine and Ranger's sleek coat shone. He and his detachment met the major about three miles out from the fort. There was no mistaking the major. He sat on his black horse with stiff, military bearing, and his uniform was precisely brushed and neat.

Rand saluted. "Good morning, sir. I'm Lieutenant Campbell

and I'm pleased to escort you to Fort Laramie."

The major saluted smartly. "At ease, Lieutenant." He dismounted and motioned for Rand to do the same. "How's the situation with the Indians? Any trouble brewing?"

"Nothing I can put my finger on, sir. But I have an uneasy feeling that something's going on we can't see right now. There have been grumblings about the miners tramping through the Sioux hunting grounds on the Bozeman Trail. Red Cloud hasn't come in for rations and some of our tame Oglala say he's calling for a fight to the knife. I don't trust him."

The major waved his hand dismissively. "We'll deal with him if he steps out of line."

The flap to the ambulance behind them opened and a young woman stepped through the opening. "Good morning, Daddy. Why have we stopped? Are we there?"

The major smiled indulgently. "Lieutenant, I'd like you to meet my daughter, Jessica. And my wife, Mrs. DuBois. Jessica, Letty, this is Lieutenant Rand Campbell. He has come to escort us into the fort."

"Call me Letty, dear," the older woman, a softer, plumper version of the daughter murmured as she placed her round hand in Rand's.

Rand gripped it briefly and muttered some response, but his gaze was on the major's daughter. She was the most beautiful woman he'd ever seen. Her fiery red hair was arranged in a mass of curls that framed her delicate face in a halo of color. She smiled at him as though he was the first man she'd ever seen.

"I'm *very* pleased to meet you," she said softly. Her soft hand lingered on his.

Rand was aware he was staring, but he couldn't seem to stop. She really was the most amazing looking woman, he thought as he helped her back up into the ambulance. He told the private driving the ambulance to take Ranger and he would drive the ladies into the fort. All the while he was conscious of Jessica's blue eyes fastened on him. Wait until Isaac saw her, he thought as she settled down beside him on the seat.

ਫ

Sarah sat by the gurgling water with the autumn sun warm on her arms. In spite of the mild temperature, Sarah couldn't seem to feel anything but a cold deadness inside. She threw stale bread to the ducks along the riverbank as she stared across the water. Why had God allowed this to happen to her? Did He really not love her as she'd told Pastor Stevens? She slid to the ground and lay back in the grass. Gazing into the sky always filled her with a sense of God's power. Tears leaked from her eyes as she thought about the mess her life was in. "Are You there, God?" she whispered. Taking her life into her own hands had certainly left it a mess.

Pastor Stevens's sermon from that morning echoed in her head. *Come unto Me, all ye that labor and are heavy laden, and I will give you rest.* She rolled over onto her stomach and didn't try to stop the tears from flowing. She wanted rest so badly. "Forgive me, Lord," she sobbed. "I've been so pigheaded and willful. I know You want only what's best for me. Help me to always see Your hand in my life. Restore me and give me Your peace. I know I fail You so many times, but I want to serve You. Wipe away my sins and let me start fresh and anew with You again."

As she prayed she felt His gentle touch in her heart. The lethargy and deadness fell away, and for the first time in two weeks, she felt hope. God was in control. Whatever He wanted was for her own good.

She sat up and wiped her eyes. She should have swallowed her pride and turned to the Lord months ago. She smiled and lifted her heavy hair from her neck for the cool breeze to caress before settling herself on the large rock again.

She sat there in quiet joy for some time before she realized she was being watched. "Papa, you startled me." She looked at him with new eyes, seeing his frailty and the yellow pallor of his skin. *He's aged so much,* she thought suddenly.

William was wheezing by the time he reached her. "Room for two?" he asked.

She moved over and he dropped down beside her. They sat in silence for a while, then he took her hand. "Is that a smile I see on your face, Sweetheart? I don't think I've seen you smile since Rand left."

Sarah kissed him on the cheek. "I've just taken Pastor Stevens's advice to heart," she said. "I've been blaming God for everything that goes wrong, and I finally saw how wrong I was. God's forgiven me, though."

Her father hugged her. "I knew you'd been bitter, but I left it for God to deal with you. That pride of yours always trips you up. You should have gone with Rand, you know. I love you, Sweetheart, but you must ask God to channel that stubbornness of yours."

Sarah looked at him in shock. "I couldn't leave you!"

"You're not a little girl anymore. And there comes a time in every person's life when he has to step out and stand on his own feet. Rand was ready, and I think you are, too. We both know I won't be around much longer."

"No, Papa—!"

He held up a hand at her protest. "You just don't want to admit it, my dear girl. I would rest easier if I knew you were settled and happy. I never expected you to give up without a fight! You had to fight to get him in the first place. Remember all the tears until I let you put your hair up and wear your mother's green satin dress for Christmas dinner with the Campbells the year you turned sixteen?"

Sarah smiled at the memory. "It worked, too. That was the first time he saw me as anything but a pesky younger sister. But he's half a continent away now. What can I do?" Tears started into her eyes, and she brushed them away angrily.

William stood up. "I don't know the answer, but I'm sure

God will tell you if you'll listen." He patted the top of her head and turned to walk back to the house.

Sarah was barely aware of his departure as a seed of an idea began to take shape. *I could follow Rand!* She almost gasped aloud at the daring thought. Women went west all the time. She could take a train to rail's end in Omaha. Surely there would be a stage or a wagon train she could catch on to Fort Leavenworth. Amelia said Jacob had told her Rand would be there until spring came. Maybe then Rand would realize how much she loved him and she could talk him into coming back home. Just for a while, of course. Just until Papa didn't need her. Of course, he wasn't dying now. He was very sick, though. But with Rand around to talk to, he'd soon recover his spirits.

But could she do it alone? What about the rough men one encountered on the frontier? She wouldn't have a protector. She smiled then. Yes, she would. God would go with her.

She spent the next two hours in feverish plans. She wished she had a pencil and paper to make a list of what she wanted to take. How long did it take to get to Fort Leavenworth, anyway? But it didn't matter. Nothing mattered except finding Rand and persuading him to come home where he belonged. She almost skipped as she hurried back to the house to begin packing. God would work everything out.

When she reached the front yard she heard shouts and almost collided with Wade as he rushed through the door. "What is it?" She blocked his path and clutched his burly arm.

He shook off her grip angrily. "It's Pa. I hope you're satisfied. You've finally managed to kill him! I'm going after Doc." He glared at her one last time before continuing his headlong flight to the barn.

Her heart in her throat, Sarah ran into the house and found Rachel kneeling beside William's crumpled form. With a cry, Sarah flung herself down beside her father and took his hand.

"Papa, it's me," she whispered. "Don't die, please don't die. Just hold on. Wade's gone for Doc."

At her voice, William's pale lids fluttered and Sarah felt his cold fingers move. She leaned closer. "Don't try to talk. I'm here with you."

With an effort he opened his eyes and tried to smile. "Don't cry, my dear girl. Jesus is waiting for me, and I'm going to be with your mama at last," he whispered. He had trouble focusing his eyes, but finally they fastened on Sarah's white face. "Just be happy, Sweetheart. You fight for your Rand, if you must, and don't let Wade bully you into anything." He coughed weakly. "But don't leave Joel with Wade. Promise me." His voice grew stronger and he raised his head slightly. "Promise!"

"I promise," Sarah whispered as she felt his icy fingers loosen.

His eyes widened. "Kate!" he gasped. His chest hitched once, then was still as the last of his breath sighed out his slightly open mouth.

"Papa!" Sarah stared at him. This couldn't be real. He'd just been talking with her! She clutched his hand tighter. "Don't leave me, Papa!" She kissed his cheek and gathered his head into her lap. "Dear God, no," she sobbed. "Don't take him. This can't be happening." She looked over at Rachel kneeling and weeping on the other side of William's body. "He's just unconscious, Rachel. He can't be dead." She felt as though she were in the grip of a nightmare and couldn't wake up. She struggled to catch her breath and shook her head slightly to clear it.

Rachel just shook her head and cried hard. "I'm so sorry, Sarah. We all loved him. He was a good man." She scooted around and put her arm around Sarah's shaking shoulders. "He never got over missing your mama. Just be happy he's finally with her again."

"But I still need him." Sarah's voice was bewildered as she

stared down into her father's peaceful face. "He can't leave me now." She touched his grizzled cheek, already cooling. *Doc will save him,* she thought.

They both turned as Wade and Doc Seth rushed in the door. "Help him, Doc," Sarah pleaded as the doctor knelt beside his friend of nearly forty years and put the stethoscope to William's chest.

There was a long pause, then the doctor straightened up. "I'm sorry, Sarah. He's gone." His voice was hoarse with emotion. William had been his best friend since he'd moved to this valley.

The words hammered into Sarah's brain with a stunning force. Wade's accusing stare was the last thing she saw before she whirled and ran from the room, keening in grief.

The next few days were hazy with anguish. There was the preparation of William's body, the ordering of the casket, the sitting up with her dead father three nights in a row, as well as the hordes of mourning friends who came to pay their last respects. William had been a much loved and respected man in the community.

Sarah thought if she heard just one more time how wonderful it was that William was finally with Kate, she would have a screaming fit. She knew she was selfish, but she wanted him here with her. Amelia hovered anxiously near her every moment, but there was nothing anyone could do to ease her grief. Pastor Stevens tried to comfort her, but she just brushed his words away.

Finally the crowds were gone, and William was laid to rest next to his beloved Kate in the meadow beneath the weeping willow tree. Sarah performed all the usual tasks of homemaking, somehow managing to get through each day. The thought of following Rand was distant and unreal. It took all her strength just to survive the heartache.

As the days passed, Sarah found herself leaning on her faith in a way she'd never known. Instead of questioning God's hand in her life, she felt His presence in a very special way. She spent many hours beneath the willow tree talking to Him as she kept vigil beside her father's grave. A week after his death, she knelt beside the two precious graves and planted bright cushions of mums over the moist mound of dirt. They reminded her that her father was more alive than he'd ever been here on earth. There was no more pain for him. Only peace and love and wonderment as he beheld heaven and his Lord. *Guide me with Your Holy Spirit, Lord,* she prayed. *Don't let me stray from the path You have chosen for me. Keep watch over Rand and send someone to speak to him about his need for You in his life.*

Sarah's twentieth birthday came and went with little festivity, just an aching sense of loss. The Montgomery home had become a solemn place where no one smiled or laughed. Jacob and Amelia slipped away and were married quietly instead of the big celebration they'd planned. Sarah stood up with Amelia, but she was still in such pain she didn't remember much about the wedding.

Six days after the wedding, she sat peeling potatoes for supper. The weather was still unseasonably warm and the breeze blew in through the open window with a hint of rain in it. The kitchen door banged, and Wade stomped in.

"Supper's not done yet?" he growled as he hung up his red plaid jacket. He turned and saw her strained face. "I think it's time you and I had a talk." His gruff voice softened as he sat down beside her.

She didn't trust his mild tone. He wanted something from her, and she had a sinking feeling she knew what it was. He'd brought up Ben's name several times over the past few weeks. "What about?" she asked quietly.

"Your future." He stared at her challengingly. "I saw Ben in town today and for some reason he still wants to marry you. I told him I didn't see any reason why you wouldn't. That good-for-nothing Campbell went off and left you in the lurch and—"

"No." The short, clipped word cut him off just as he was picking up steam.

"You will do what I say. You're under age and my ward." Wade compressed his lips in an effort to keep his temper.

"I will *not* marry Ben. Rand and I belong together. That was Papa's last words to me. I won't marry anyone but Rand. I'll never marry Ben."

"Well, that's just too bad, missy. You'd better get used to the idea because you will do as I say. Campbell has run off to the frontier, and you'll never see him again anyway." He pulled her to her feet and shoved her toward the door. "You'll stay in your room until you agree to abide by my decisions." He grabbed her arm and dragged her ruthlessly up the stairs and into her room.

Sarah stared at the closed door in disbelief as the lock clicked shut behind her brother. His behavior had shocked her so much she hadn't put up much fight. "You can't keep me in here, Wade," she shouted. "This isn't the Middle Ages!" She heard his heavy tread down the steps and ran to the door. "Let me out of here. I'll never marry Ben—never!" She twisted the latch to no avail, then kicked at the solid oak door in a helpless frenzy of rage. Minutes later she had nothing to show for her efforts except a sore foot and a splinter in the palm of her hand.

She sat down on the bed to think. Joel would be home soon, and Rachel would be back from the market. Surely one of them could be persuaded to let her out. But what then? What could she do? She bit her lip. The idea of going to Rand revived suddenly. Jacob and Amelia were leaving tomorrow. Perhaps she could convince them to let her go out with them. Jacob would surely be glad of a companion for Amelia. She'd find Rand and confess how wrong she'd been. Surely he would forgive her. They could make a new life away from Wade's meddling.

Instead of asking to be let out, she spent the night planning her escape and was pale and drawn from lack of sleep by the time morning came. She packed a suitcase of essentials and hid it under the bed just as she heard Wade's heavy tread outside the door.

The lock turned and he stepped into the room. She wanted to throw something at him as soon as she saw his smug face. "Ready to be reasonable yet?"

"Do I have a choice?" she kept her face averted so he couldn't see her eyes.

He smiled. He hadn't expected such an early capitulation. "I knew you'd come around. I had Rachel save you some breakfast."

The exultation in his voice caused her to clench her hands to keep from screaming at him. "I'm not hungry," she said quietly.

He eyed her bent head, then satisfied that he'd broken her spirit, just nodded. "Fine. I'll go talk to Pastor Stevens, and we'll discuss when the wedding can take place." He left the door open behind him and tromped back downstairs and out the door.

She sprang to her feet as soon as she heard the buggy rumble down the rutted track toward town. Feverishly she pulled her suitcase from under her bed. As she picked it up and turned toward the door, she heard someone in the hall. She froze until she realized it was just Joel.

"What are you doing?" Joel's face was pinched and drawn with misery. His red hair didn't look as though it had been combed for days. He'd had a rough time these last few weeks, too. He as well as Sarah had lost his father. She'd been too overcome with grief to pay much attention to him.

Sarah stared at him in consternation. She had forgotten about Joel and her promise to her father. She couldn't leave him here with Wade. She knelt and put her arms around him. "I'm going to find Rand, and I want you to come with me."

His pale face brightened. "Honest Injun?"

"Honest Injun." How she was going to manage it, she wasn't quite sure, but she'd find a way. It would be hard enough to slip away by herself, but encumbered by an eleven-year-old, it would be much harder. "Let's hurry and pack your things before Wade gets back."

They hurried to Joel's room and Sarah threw three changes of clothes for him in the only suitcase small enough for him to handle.

"Can I take my rifle?"

Sarah hesitated as she looked into his pleading face. The less baggage the better, but the rifle had been Papa's and she didn't have the heart to make him leave it behind. She nodded and he slung it over his shoulder and picked up his suitcase. They slipped down the steps and came face to face with Rachel.

She looked from the suitcases to Sarah's face. "You're leaving." It wasn't a question. "I knew Wade would never force you to fall in with his plans—but who has ever been able to tell him anything?" She pushed her hair back from her forehead and held out her arms.

Sarah put down her suitcase and went to Rachel with a sigh. "I'll miss you, Rachel. But I have to find Rand." Her words were muffled against Rachel's shoulder. She drew away and looked into her sister-in-law's eyes. "Don't tell Wade I've gone."

Rachel smiled faintly. "No problem. He won't be back till suppertime. If you hurry, you can catch the afternoon train and be long gone before he knows you've left." She hugged her fiercely, then shoved her toward the door. "Write when you get there. And don't forget about me and the baby. We love you."

Sarah gulped and wiped her eyes. "I know, Rachel. And you've been a real sister to me. Make sure you write us when the baby's born."

Rachel nodded, then smiled through her tears and made a

shooing motion with her apron. "You'd best get going. You have a lot to get done today."

Joel hurried ahead to hitch up the buggy while Sarah took one last look at the home where she'd been born. The sun shone through the bare trees in dappled patterns on the front porch roof. The solid two-story seemed so safe and familiar. She could see the red barn just behind it where she'd played in the haymow as a child. The chicken coop off to the east, the pasture beyond that, and all around the gently rolling hills of Montgomery land; it was all so heartbreakingly beloved.

She'd never had any plans of leaving her home. At least not any farther than the knoll beyond the pasture. Would she ever see it again? And who would tend Papa's grave?

She choked back tears and climbed up beside Joel. This was no time for tears, for second thoughts. Wade had left her no choice. She waved one last good-bye at Rachel, then stared firmly ahead. She couldn't think about what she was leaving or she wouldn't be able to go.

eight

Sarah stared unseeingly out the window of the stagecoach as the barren landscape swept by. Would this trip never end? Jacob and Amelia had readily fallen in with her plan. They had assumed she was arriving to say good-bye, and Amelia's sad little face had flushed with joy when she realized her best friend would be coming with them. By ten o'clock the four of them were on the train headed west.

When they arrived at Leavenworth, they'd found Rand had gone on to Laramie. It was just a temporary setback, though, as the commander readily agreed to allow Jacob to accompany a troop of new recruits heading out to Laramie. Four days later they squeezed about the crowded stagecoach and started the last eighty miles of their journey. Sarah's teeth chattered as the unheated stagecoach lurched and bounced its way across the frozen prairie. They were all crammed together so tightly she couldn't move anything except her head, and every bone in her body ached. She could no longer remember a time when she wasn't cold and sore.

The smell bothered Sarah and Amelia more than anything. The stagecoach reeked of dusty leather, hair tonic, horse, and underlying everything else, the unlovely aroma of unwashed bodies. Occasionally, several of the soldiers traveling with them tried to strike up a conversation, but they soon fell silent under Jacob's glowering gaze.

The frozen landscape rolled past all that day and through the night. The next morning was colder, and a hint of moisture was in the blustery wind. The soldiers predicted a blizzard but not until the next day. They should all be safe and snug in Fort Laramie by then.

"I can't believe we missed Rand. He wasn't supposed to come out to this wilderness until spring," Sarah moaned.

"It won't be long now," Amelia said soothingly.

Sarah sighed again and her breath steamed. "I hope I get a chance to bathe before I see Rand. I must look terrible." She could feel her hair hanging in straggly wisps against her cheeks. The last time she pushed it out of her face, her gloves had come away smeared with dirt. Rand would take one look at her and send her home.

Jacob shuffled his feet on the other side of Amelia as the driver gave a shout from topside. He grinned at Sarah. "Sounds like we're there."

Sarah moaned and tried to pat the strands of hair back into some semblance of order as she lifted the leather covering and peered out of the window at the famous fort. Surrounded by rocky soil and sagebrush, it sprawled across the Laramie River, its frame and adobe buildings lining a wide parade ground fortified with mountain howitzers. But it was all so barren. The fort seemed a tiny oasis in a vast plain of frigid wasteland.

She gave an involuntary gasp when she saw the Indians encamped all around the fort, their teepees gleaming in the sunshine. Hundreds of them. Squaws squatted around open fires; children shouted and played in the dust.

"The fort's been overrun with Indians," she gulped.

The garrulous old soldier across the aisle chuckled. "Fort Laramie's the headquarters for the Sioux. There's always a passel of redskins 'round here. You'll git used to it."

"But there's no stockade," she said with a shudder. "What if they turn hostile?"

"There's always plenty of hostiles around, but they know better than to attack a fort as well garrisoned as this one. You don't need to worry none, missy. The most them savages ever done was run howling through the pasture to stampede the horses."

Several soldiers manned a ferry, and the trip across the river was accomplished quickly. Sarah's heart pounded as the horses pulled the stage up the hill and it rolled to a stop. The driver threw open the door and helped the two ladies down before climbing on top and tossing all the luggage down to the eager hands waiting below.

Sarah stared all around in dismay. It was not at all as she'd imagined. The adobe buildings sat in neat rows along a barren parade ground. They looked cheerless and unwelcoming. A U.S. flag whipped forlornly in the wind atop a flagpole on the far side of the parade ground. The fort seemed to be stuck out in the middle of nowhere with the wilderness all around. She could feel all the soldiers milling around the fort staring at her and Amelia.

"It'll look better come spring," the old soldier consoled.

Jacob piled their luggage together in a heap, then accosted a nearby soldier. "Could you tell me where we might find Captain Rand Campbell?"

"Well don't this beat the Dutch." The soldier had a friendly, smiling face. "You've gotta be Jacob. You look enough like your brother to be two peas out of the same pod." The soldier stuck out a large callused hand. "Isaac Liddle's my name, and Rand's my bunky."

Jacob shook his hand vigorously. "Mighty glad to meet you. Got any idea where that rascal brother of mine is?"

"Probably at mess. Bugle sounded a few minutes ago. I was headed there myself. Just follow me."

Shivering as much from nerves as from the cold, Sarah took Joel's hand and trailed behind Jacob and Amelia. She felt as though her entire future hung in the balance. She could hear shouts of laughter emanating from the officer's mess hall, and her stomach rumbled hungrily as the wind brought a mouth-watering aroma of stew to her nose.

The room was brightly lit with dozens of lanterns and the general feeling of high spirits and fellowship warmed her as much as the heat rolling from the pot-bellied stove in the center of the room. Her green eyes scanned the room quickly as their presence in the room caused the babble of voices to soften, then still. She caught sight of Rand sitting at the far table next to two women. Her first impulse was to call out his name and run to him, but the expression on his face as he gazed at the young redheaded woman stopped her. Sarah didn't like the dazed smile on his face or the possessive hand the woman had on his arm. She gulped as he looked up and saw them.

Rand rose slowly to his feet as the small party neared. "Sarah? And Jacob! I didn't expect you, Jacob, not for at least another week or two." He grabbed his brother's hand and pumped it, then hugged Amelia and Joel but didn't touch Sarah. "Hello, Sarah."

"Who are all these folks, Rand?" The redheaded woman stood and slid her hand into the crook of Rand's arm, and Sarah caught a whiff of her perfume. Some exotic flowery scent she couldn't place. "Introduce me to your friends," the woman purred.

"Jessica, this is my brother Jacob, his wife Amelia, and," he hesitated, then continued. "And some friends from back home, Sarah Montgomery and her brother Joel."

"Pleased to meet you all," Jessica said with a seductive smile. "I've heard all about you, Jacob. Rand tells me you're the county boxing champion." Her smile deepened into a dimple as she looked at Jacob. "I'm Jessica DuBois and this is my mother, Mrs. Major DuBois."

The address sounded strange to Sarah, but she was aware that was how wives were addressed in the army. And Sarah thought she'd never seen anyone more lovely than the young woman on Rand's arm. Jessica had deep blue eyes and deep red hair that shimmered in the candlelight. Her skin was almost translucent, with a pale pink tint to her high cheekbones and full lips. Jessica's mother was a blurred image of her daughter with softer, plumper lines and a gentle expression.

"Please call me Letty, dear," the older woman murmured. "Everyone does." She smiled at Amelia and Sarah. "I'm so glad to have two other women here at Laramie. We must get together for tea tomorrow. We ladies have to stick together. It helps the time go by. And you all are here just in time to help plan the wedding."

"Wedding?" Sarah looked at Rand. "Whose wedding?"

"Why mine and Rand's, of course." Jessica hit Rand on the arm with her fan. "Why, you bad boy, haven't you told your family about us yet?"

"They had probably left Wabash by the time my letter got there," Rand said, his eyes on Sarah's face.

Sarah felt as though she were falling. She couldn't catch her breath. How could he? How could he come out and get engaged in less than two months? She fought down the tight tears in her throat as she gripped Amelia's hand. She didn't want to give the other woman the satisfaction of seeing her cry. Did she know Sarah had once been engaged to Rand?

"Congratulations," Jacob said after an awkward pause. "I had no idea you were seeing anyone, Rand."

"I think a kiss for your new sister-in-law-to-be is in order," Jessica said. She stood on her tiptoes and kissed Jacob lingeringly on the lips. Sarah saw Amelia clench her jaw.

"Rand, we're really tired," Amelia said through tight lips. "Could you see about finding us a place to stay tonight?"

"The quartermaster is by the door. Come with me, Jacob, and we'll get you all fixed up."

"My goodness," Jessica said as the men walked away. "You and I are certainly lucky ladies, Amelia. Those are some men we have." She didn't seem aware of the undercurrent of tension as she turned to Sarah. "Have you known Rand long yourself? I knew as soon as I set eyes on him, I was going to marry him."

"All my life," Sarah said, ignoring her last statement.

Joel tugged on Sarah's arm. "How can Rand marry that

lady when he's going to marry you?"

Jessica choked on her coffee. "Why, whatever does the boy mean?" she asked.

Sarah went scarlet with mortification. She had wanted to preserve her dignity if she could. "Rand and I were engaged before the war," she admitted.

"Oh, I see," Jessica said with a long look at Sarah's face. She narrowed her eyes. "You lost him. Well, let me tell you, I don't intend to lose him. Don't think you can waltz in here and take him back. We're getting married in June, and I won't allow anyone or anything to interfere with my plans."

Sarah gasped and choked back an angry retort. She was a new creature now, she had to remind herself. God was in control of this situation, too. "Rand and I have been friends all our lives," she said quietly. "If you are the woman he wants, I want to be friends with you, too." She could sense Amelia's silent approval of her soft answer.

Jessica frowned, uncertain how to respond to the gentle answer. "Well, uhm, that's fine then," she finally muttered ungraciously as Jacob hurried back over to them.

"We're all fixed up," Jacob announced. "Let's go get settled. Rand is going to bring us over some stew after we get cleaned up."

"You just remember what I said," Jessica murmured as Sarah turned to follow the men out of the mess hall. "I never give up anything that belongs to me." She flounced back to the table with her mother.

Sarah felt numb as she held onto her skirts and followed the little party across the windy parade ground. How could all her hopes and dreams end like this? What could she do? Was this God's plan?

Rand led them to an adobe building. "Captain Leeks lives on the other side with his family, but his family never stays here in the winter. His wife and two sons will be back in May." He opened the door and led them into a narrow hall that opened onto a small, cheerless parlor. The room was cold and barren with plain plank floors. It smelled musty from disuse but had a lingering odor of smoke and soot. Rand knelt at the fireplace and poked at the logs. "I'll have it warmed up in no time." He got the fire going, then stood. "I'll leave you to get cleaned up. I'll be back in about an hour with some supper for you." He grinned. "Cooky likes me. When he hears we have two new ladies, he'll be glad to whip up something."

"We need to talk," Sarah said. She stared at him, her green eyes direct.

Rand avoided her eyes. "I'll be back later. We'll talk then."

"Now, please."

Rand sighed and ran his hand through his hair. "Sarah, you need to unpack and get settled in. And we need to talk in private."

He was right, Sarah knew. She sighed and turned away. She knew it was a vain hope to think there might be some good explanation for what had happened. Rand was engaged to another woman. What was there to explain? It was pretty self-explanatory. No wonder he wasn't anxious to discuss it with her. Was this the same man she'd known all her life?

In the tiny kitchen there was a Sibley stove that Jacob soon had blazing. The warmth crept into the room and seeped into Sarah's cold skin, but nothing could reach the icy despair in her heart. A battered kettle sat on the stove. Sarah rinsed it with water from the bucket a private brought to the back door. First they'd have a cup of tea and then see to bathing the road dust off their sore bodies. She felt as though the fine yellow grit was in every pore of her body. She could even taste its gritty presence in her throat. She looked around the small quarters. Only one small bedroom opened off the kitchen. Where could they all sleep?

"I'll bring over a couple more bunks," Jacob said. "We can put one in the parlor and use it for a sofa during the day. You can sleep there, Sarah. I'll put another one in the entry for

Joel, and everyone will have a little privacy. Just for tonight, you and Amelia can sleep in the bedroom, and Joel and I will put up in the barracks." He hauled the hip bath down off its peg on the wall and set it in the small bedroom. He sent the private down to the river to haul some more water for bathing.

Even with several kettles of boiling water added, the bath water was barely tepid, so they all bathed quickly. They were all ravenous by the time Rand brought over a steaming kettle of stew and bread. They wolfed down their supper in ten minutes.

Jacob yawned. "I'm beat. I think the rest of us will turn in if you and Sarah want to talk, Rand."

Rand nodded reluctantly. "See you in the morning," he said.

"Can I look at your saber?" Joel asked between yawns.

"In the morning." Rand grinned at Joel's crestfallen expression and ruffled his hair. "You guys get some sleep. When you're rested, I'll show you around your new home tomorrow."

Joel and Jacob said a quick farewell and headed out for the barracks. Amelia smiled encouragingly at Sarah before slipping off to the bedroom. Sarah waited until the door to the bedroom was closed, then turned her green eyes up to Rand. "How could you do this, Rand? It hasn't even been two months since you asked me to come out here with you. Does your love die so quickly?" The pent-up hurt and betrayal burst out of her before she could consider her words.

Rand raked a hand through his hair and sighed deeply. He tightened his lips and squared his shoulders before answering. "I like army life, Sarah. The adventure, the sense of doing something worthwhile with my life. Something that affects other people besides just my family. I want to be part of taming the West for my country. And Jessica will make an excellent army wife. She's lived on frontier forts most of her life. It hurt when you didn't love me enough to leave your family for me. Jessica will go wherever I'm sent without a complaint. She understands soldiers and their duties."

"You can't tell me this is just a marriage of convenience! I saw the way you were looking at her when we arrived. And if you are just using her, what kind of a man have you turned into, Rand?"

"I care about her," Rand admitted. "She was here when I was hurting over your rejection. She let me know right off how she felt. I needed someone and she was there. And like I said, she'll make a good army wife. What are you doing here, anyway? You said you'd never leave Indiana."

"Papa's dead." She regretted her bald words as soon as she saw the hurt and shock register on his face. She softened her tone. "His heart just—gave out."

"Oh, Sarah." He ran a hand through his thick hair. "I really loved your pa. He was like a father to me."

"He loved you, too," she said softly. "He spoke of you just before he died."

"He did?"

She nodded. "He was gone just a few minutes after we'd talked. He told me—" She broke off and bit her lip.

"He told you what?"

"He urged me to fight for you."

Rand sighed. "Is that why you're here? Now that he's gone and you don't have anything else to do?"

Sarah bit her lip. What should she tell him? Slowly she nodded. "I was coming before he died. I was making plans when I heard the shouts at the house. His death actually delayed my arrival by several weeks."

"You're a little late."

"So I see," she said. "You're not the same man I've loved for so long. Where did he go?"

"He died in the war," Rand said stiffly.

Sarah laid a hand on his arm. "Rand, you won't be happy with this kind of life. I've discovered in the past few weeks how important it is to let God lead me. If I hadn't been determined to run my own life, I wouldn't have been deceived by Ben."

"You sound like Isaac," Rand blurted before he could stop himself.

"Isaac is a Christian?" she asked.

He nodded. "He's been a good friend. And I have to admit I sometimes wonder what's the right thing to do with my life. But I don't think God bothers with our daily lives. I believe He's out there somewhere, but I don't think He cares what we do. We just use our own ingenuity to live our lives as best we can."

Sarah shook her head. "Your grandma would wallop you if she heard you say such a thing."

Rand grinned. "Probably. But it's how I feel. If God ever speaks to me directly, maybe I'll listen."

"It may be too late, then."

"I'll just have to take that chance," he said firmly.

"Do you love Jessica?" Her face felt so stiff she could barely move her lips. She had to know the answer, but her heart pounded with fear.

"Not like I loved you. But she's been good to me. And she's very sweet and kind. I can't just throw her off like a busted saddle."

Sarah stared at him incredulously. Sweet and kind? He must see something she didn't. "Then there's nothing more to say. I'll try not to bother you too much. You'd better go now." Her eyes burning with tears, she stepped away.

He hesitated, then nodded. "I guess you're right. I'm sorry, Green Eyes."

Don't call me that, she wanted to shout. *You're not the same man who nicknamed me that.* But she said nothing. He picked up his coat and left silently. As the door shut behind him, she let tears fall.

nine

Reveille sounded at five, but Rand was already awake. Jacob and Joel were sleepily pulling on their overalls and boots when he strode in to check on them. "Hurry up or you'll miss the cold slop we call breakfast," Rand said with a grin.

"How's the Indian situation?" Jacob poured icy water out of a battered tin pitcher into a chipped bowl and splashed his eyes, bleary from lack of sleep. A group of soldiers had been up playing cards all night, and their loud talk and laughter had made sleep difficult. Most of them had already cleared out of the long room lined with bunks, but the odor of hair tonic and dirty socks still lingered.

"Bad. And likely to get worse. The Bureau of Indian Affairs has really botched things. Every agent they've sent sets out to line his pockets with what belongs to the Indians. Once one gets rich enough, he goes back east and another comes to start the same process all over again." Rand shook his head. "And it's really explosive up in the Powder River area. Quite a few miners have been killed trying to get to the gold fields."

"Much hostility around here?"

"Not really. A few skirmishes. There's mostly tame Oglala Sioux and friendly Brule'. Most of the wild Oglala are with Red Cloud at Powder River."

"The girls will be relieved to hear that."

"I was just about to check on them." Rand paused. "I'm sure glad you're here, Big Jacob. You're going to love this country."

The smell of impending snow freshened the air and the frigid wind stung their cheeks as they hurried across the parade ground toward the light spilling out the front window

84

of the house. It looked warm and welcoming in the somber darkness of the predawn morning. Their breath made frosty plumes in the air, and their boots crunched against the frozen ground as they waved and called morning greetings to the soldiers heading toward the mess hall, most of them shrouded in buffalo robes against the cold. The trumpet's call to breakfast carried clearly in the cold, clear air.

≈

Sarah's heart was heavy as she finished dressing. Rand and Jacob should be here any moment and she didn't know how she should act. She wasn't sure what she should do. She couldn't go back home. Wade would just get up to his old tricks again. She turned as she heard the men thump up the porch steps and ran to unlock the door. "Good morning," she smiled, anxiously searching Rand's face.

Rand avoided her eyes. "Breakfast is going to be over if you two don't hurry up."

"We're almost ready. Let me finish my hair. Jacob, why don't you take Amelia and Joel and go on ahead?" Sarah's words were mumbled through a mouthful of hairpins. She had deliberately dawdled over her toilet so she might have a few moments alone with Rand.

With a quick, understanding glance, Amelia drew on her navy cape and followed Jacob and Joel out the door. Sarah finished her hair with a few quick thrusts of well-placed hairpins, then looked up at Rand. "Have you thought about what we talked about last night?"

"Sarah, what do you want me to say? It's too late. All the regrets in the world won't change the situation." He looked away and swallowed hard. "We both know it's over. Unless of course you're looking for a new fellow." He clipped the words out. "There's plenty willing I'm sure. It's so rare for the men to see any unattached women—you'll probably have a dozen proposals before the week is over."

Stung by his words, Sarah tossed her head. "Don't worry

that I'm going to embarrass you with unwanted attentions. I had hoped we could at least be friends."

"As long as you don't expect anything more from me. Jacob said he'd probably be sent to one of the northern forts come late spring or early summer, so I reckon we can be civil to one another for a few months." He picked up her cloak from the foot of the bed and held it out to her courteously. "Now I think we'd best be heading over to mess. As I recall, you're always hungry in the morning—unless that's changed, too."

Red spots bloomed in Sarah's cheeks and her lips tightened. "I'm not the one who's changed—you have! Traipsing off to the back of beyond was never in our plans. Where's the gentle farmer I used to know? The Rand I knew wasn't a glory-hungry warrior." She drew her gloves on with angry jerks and tied her bonnet under her chin. Her green eyes sparkled with suppressed fury.

Rand shrugged. "Maybe so. But I'm not the same person I was before the war. And neither are you, in spite of your not wanting to admit it."

She swished away from him without another word. The wind struck her as she stepped out onto the porch, and as she staggered, Rand caught her arm and steadied her. She was very conscious of his strong, warm fingers pressing against her arm through her cape.

His dark eyes were impersonal as he gazed down on her. "The wind is ferocious out here. Watch your step." He led her across the parade ground toward the mess hall, the soft glow of lamp light shining out its windows and a lazy curl of smoke rising from its chimney.

With an effort Sarah controlled her hurt and anger. She forced a smile to her face and laid a hand on his arm before stepping into the mess hall. "I'm sorry I lost my temper. Friends?"

Rand hesitated, then smiled. "Friends." He closed the door firmly against the rising wind outside.

The mess hall was a big open room filled with long wooden tables that seated eight to ten men. The tables closest to the stove in the center of the room were all filled. "Rand!" Jessica, clad in a green dress, was seated across the table from Jacob, Amelia, and Joel at the table closest to the stove. She waved to them.

Sarah stifled a sigh. She hadn't thought she'd have to face Jessica quite so soon. The other woman's shining red hair was elegantly piled high on her head, and her pale complexion was flawless. Her mother had the same cool loveliness, but where her expression was serene and gentle, her daughter had a petulant twist to her mouth and an acquisitive look in her blue eyes.

Jessica nodded coolly, then turned adoring eyes up to Rand. "Don't forget the new play at Bedlam is tonight. You did say you'd pick me up at seven, right?"

Rand nodded and Sarah clenched her fists in the folds of her skirt until the overwhelming jealousy subsided.

"You must come, Miss Montgomery. You and your friends." Mrs. DuBois fluttered her plump, white hands. "My husband has the lead role, and you'll be able to meet all the officers."

"Please call me Sarah," she said automatically, her eyes on Rand and Jessica.

"You can call me Letty. Everyone does, my dear. It will be so pleasant to have other ladies at the fort." She shuddered delicately. "One gets so lonesome for the refined company of other women in this primitive place. Perhaps we can get together for tea tomorrow?"

Sarah forced herself to smile and accept Letty's invitation as she strained her ears to listen to Jessica's monopoly of Rand's conversation. Obviously, Rand had spent considerable time with this girl and enjoyed her company. Did Rand really love her? But no. Sarah refused to believe that. They had shared too much and their love was too strong for it to just die like that. She *would* get through to Rand; she wasn't too late. Sooner or later he would realize he really loved her. God wouldn't have brought her this far for it all to end.

But what if He had? Maybe He had other plans for her. He certainly wouldn't want her to marry Rand when he held beliefs so contrary to God's Word. She felt weary and defeated as she settled down to eat breakfast.

The breakfast lasted an interminable amount of time as they ate the nearly cold flapjacks and grits and washed it all down with strong, hot coffee. Nearly every officer in the place found some excuse to stop at their table for an introduction. Jacob glowered at the attention Amelia received, but Rand just looked on impassively as the younger officers flirted with Sarah and paid her extravagant compliments.

Jessica made no attempt to hide her disinterest in any man except for Rand. She glared after them when Rand told them he was taking the new arrivals on a tour of the fort and took his leave of her and her mother. Sarah resisted the urge to give Jessica a triumphant smile. Anyway, she felt anything but triumph. She wanted Rand's love, not his duty.

After breakfast the quartermaster gave them rough woolen blankets, a couple of crude wooden beds with straw mattresses, and a water bucket. Amelia had brought a trunk packed with kitchen utensils and plates as well as some bright calico and gingham material, several sets of muslin sheets, and some quilts she'd made over the years.

As they carried their booty back to their quarters, Sarah was able to take a good look at their new home. Darkness had fallen so quickly last night she hadn't really noticed much about it. A front porch ran the width of the house with wide front steps. Two doors opened off the unpainted porch.

Rand opened the main door, and they stepped inside the wide, bare entry hall. The first door led to the tiny sitting room that looked out on the front porch. Sarah stood looking around with her hands on her hips. There were definite possibilities.

She walked through the narrow door in the small kitchen and surveyed the Sibley stove in the middle of the tiny room. There was just enough space in the corner for a small table. Hooks could be hung from the low roof for pots and a small corner cupboard could be built in the corner adjoining the parlor. "What do you think, Amelia?"

Amelia brushed a stray wisp of hair out of her eyes. "I don't know where to begin," she faltered. "You take charge, Sarah. You're so much better at decisions than I am."

By midafternoon the tiny rooms had been scrubbed, Jacob had tacked the wool blankets to the floor in the sitting room and bedroom, fires blazed in all three fireplaces, and the beds were set up and ready for occupancy. Sarah and Amelia each had a lapful of material as they stitched curtains for the windows and cloths to cover the crates that would suffice as tables. Sarah could hear the thunk of axes behind the house where Joel and Jacob were chopping more wood. Isaac had told them to let the wood detail bring them more logs, but Jacob insisted he needed the exercise after being cooped up in the stage for so long. She glanced around the room in satisfaction as she sewed. They could write and ask Margaret to send a rug for the sitting room, she decided. With a few trinkets and pictures, it would be quite homey. At least it was beginning to feel like home.

ten

Sarah awoke the next morning with a sense of foreboding. What was wrong with her? she wondered. Then with a sinking heart she remembered. She and Amelia had promised Mrs. DuBois to come to tea around eleven. She groaned and pulled the blanket over her head. Maybe the weather would still be too bad to get out, she thought, remembering the fierce snowstorm that blew in late last night. But no. She could hear the bustling as the fort awakened for a new day. The wind no longer howled, and she could see a glow as the sunrise began to peek out of the eastern hills.

She groaned again. The last thing she wanted was to hear details about the wedding. And Jessica was cruel enough to delight in seeing if she could make Sarah squirm. Sarah sat up and swung her feet to the cold floor. She lifted her small, pointed chin and pressed her lips together. She'd be cool and calm. No matter what Jessica said or how much it hurt, she wouldn't let her see her pain.

By the time Amelia and Jacob opened their bedroom door, Sarah had already gone through her trunk and decided on a dress. It was a deep green poplin trimmed with black velvet and edged with lace. A sleeveless jacket of black corded silk went over the dress and cinched over her tiny waist. Her father had bought it for her from an elegant shop in Indianapolis just six months before he died. An intricate design of velvet ribbon adorned the skirt and sleeves. Sarah had always loved the dress.

"Good morning," she called when she saw Amelia and Jacob. She tested the curling tongs on the kitchen stove with a wet finger. It sizzled. Good. Almost hot enough.

"You're up early," Amelia yawned. "What's the occasion?"

"Have you forgotten we have a date for tea?"

Amelia eyed her uncertainly. "You seem almost pleased. I thought you were dreading it." She put a skillet on the stove and turned to mix up a batch of biscuits.

"Don't bother with breakfast for me," Jacob interrupted. "I'm running late. I'll grab something at officer's mess." He kissed Amelia and grabbed his coat off the hook by the stove.

"Be careful," Amelia called before turning her attention back to Sarah.

"I was really hating the thought of having to be nice to the icy queen," Sarah continued. "Then I decided it would just be a challenge. God promised us that we would be conquerors in all things. This is a chance for me to put my faith into practice. Besides, there must be some good in her or Rand wouldn't care about her."

Amelia smiled. "I wish you luck finding it. I haven't seen it yet."

"My, that doesn't sound like you. I've never known you to have a bad word to say about anyone but Ben. You're always telling me to have more patience with people."

Amelia colored. "I know I shouldn't feel that way, but she makes me uneasy just as Ben did."

"Well, she's not married to Rand yet. Could you help me with my hair? I want to look my best."

Amelia nodded and the girls spent the next hour curling Sarah's glistening red-gold locks. They pulled her heavy hair back from her heart-shaped face and let the back cascade down in tight curls. After pulling a few curls forward by her ears, Sarah was finally satisfied.

Amelia looked pretty and demure in a deep blue silk dress with a lace collar and lace around the sleeves. Her dark hair was pulled back in a loose knot at the nape of her neck with a few loose curls escaping at the sides.

Sarah threw her best cloak of brown wool with bands of

velvet fringe over her shoulder, tied on her green silk bonnet, and walked confidently toward the door with Amelia in tow. Knowing she looked her best helped calm her agitation.

But when Mrs. DuBois opened the door and Sarah saw Jessica standing behind her, she felt dowdy and plain. Jessica wore a lilac-colored silk dress with an intricate pattern in the skirt. Rows of lace ruffles cascaded over the skirt and sleeves, and her lovely white shoulders were bare. Her hair was braided and looped in an intricate way Sarah had never seen. The style accentuated Jessica's high cheekbones and big blue eyes.

But Mrs. DuBois was easy to like in spite of her daughter. "Come in, come in, my dears." She fluttered her plump hands as she drew them inside the warm hallway. "We've been so looking forward to this, haven't we, Jessica dear?"

"I certainly have."

Sarah thought she detected the hint of a sneer in Jessica's smooth voice. She squared her shoulders as she handed her cloak and bonnet to Mrs. DuBois.

Jessica led the way into their cheerily decorated quarters. Since Major DuBois was a senior officer, he received more deluxe accommodations than a lowly lieutenant. The parlor was large with a soft flowered carpet on the wood floor. Dainty tables and a horsehair sofa and three chairs furnished the room. Garden pictures and gold sconces adorned two walls while the fireplace dominated the third. Sarah could see the dining room through the arched doorway. A fine walnut table and chairs on another beautiful carpet occupied the center of the room. A young, attractive black woman hovered near the table.

"Rose, please pour our guests some tea," Mrs. DuBois called. "Sit down, ladies, and tell us how you like our little garrison."

Sarah sat on the sofa, expecting Amelia to sit next to her, but Jessica quickly settled there. With a quick glance at Sarah, Amelia sat down on one of the chairs while Mrs.

DuBois took possession of another one.

"What do you think of Fort Laramie so far? Are you ready to return to Indiana?" Mrs. DuBois asked.

"It's much more primitive than I expected," Sarah admitted. "And so cold. It seems very isolated."

"It's really very jolly in the summer. More ladies are here and we have dances and parties almost every night. Wait until then before you decide to leave us."

"They'll be gone by then, Mother. Won't you?" Jessica addressed her last remark to Sarah.

Sarah forced herself to smile breezily. "Who really knows with the army? We're hoping to stay near Rand as long as we can." She heard Jessica's sharp intake of breath.

"Excuse me for a moment, ladies," Mrs. DuBois said, seemingly unaware of the awkward pause. "I just want to peek in to see how our refreshments are coming." She scurried away and disappeared behind the door on the far side of the dining room.

As soon as her mother was gone, Jessica turned to Sarah with an angry glare. "Just what did you mean by that remark? I've already warned you not to meddle. Nothing is going to stop this wedding. You try and I promise you, you'll be very, very sorry."

"I didn't mean anything other than we all love Rand and want to be with him as long as we can. He was gone three years and only home a few days before coming out here." Sarah looked earnestly into Jessica's eyes. "I won't lie to you and tell you I don't still love him. But I want him to be happy, and if that means marriage to you, I'll try to accept that."

Jessica's face whitened as her mother came back into the room. The look she cast at Sarah was full of venom, and Sarah could see the effort it took for her to control herself in her mother's presence.

The next hour was spent in light conversation over a delicious tea of dainty chicken salad sandwiches, tiny cakes, and cookies. Sarah was aware the entire time of Jessica's seething anger just under her smooth surface.

"Do come again," Mrs. DuBois urged as she handed the girls their cloaks and bonnets. "I so enjoyed your company."

After promising they would come again, Amelia and Sarah made their escape. Amelia let out a sigh as soon as the door closed and they stepped down onto the path back home. "You've made a real enemy, Sarah. She seems capable of anything."

Sarah sighed. "I meant to try to be on friendly terms with her. I really want God's will in this, even if it means I have to give Rand up." Tears sparkled on her lashes. "It will be the hardest thing I've ever done, though."

Amelia slipped an arm around her waist as they trudged through the snow toward home. "I pray about it all the time. God will work in Rand's heart."

"I think so, too." Sarah hesitated, then continued slowly. "But if He chooses not to—or if Rand won't let him—I'll survive. That's one thing I've learned in these last few months. With God's help I can make it through anything."

Amelia smiled. "It's good to hear you talk like that." They reached their door and Joel came tearing out.

Sarah caught him as he tried to rush past them. "Whoa. What's going on?" Before Joel could answer, Rand strolled out behind him.

"We're going ice fishing," Rand said. "With your permission, of course. I was going to ask before I took him, but I wasn't sure where you were, and he assured me you wouldn't mind."

"No, of course I don't mind. And we were at the DuBois's for tea," she added as he turned to go.

He stopped and gave her a quick look. "I see," was all he said. He cleared his throat. "Well, we'll be going now. He'll be back in time for supper."

"Have fun." Her heart ached as she watched him match his

stride to Joel's shorter one. Her brother looked up at him adoringly as they walked away. Would things ever be right? Was it even possible to untangle this mess? She sighed and followed Amelia into the house. She'd try her best and leave it in God's hands. It was all she could do.

❧

A couple days later, Rand was sleeping soundly when a timid hand shook him awake.

"Captain Campbell, sir. Colonel Maynadier wants to see you right away," a young private told him.

He dismissed the private with a curt salute and pulled on his pants. What could the colonel want with him so early? Fifteen minutes later he rapped at the door leading to his commander's office.

"Enter."

He stepped inside the room, taking in the piles of papers scattered over the old wooden desk before saluting smartly. "You wanted to see me, sir?"

"Ah, yes, Captain Campbell." The colonel looked up from his scrutiny of the document in front of him. He was a tall, spare man somewhere in his forties with blond, thinning hair and pale eyebrows. But there was nothing nondescript about his eyes. They were gray and eagle sharp. The soldiers under his command knew those eyes missed nothing that concerned the well-being of Fort Laramie. Rand sometimes thought the colonel could see inside his soul with those eyes. "Camp rumor has it that a certain Lieutenant Jacob Campbell is your brother and that he arrived a few days ago with a wife and her companion. Is that correct?"

"Yes, sir."

"Excellent. I have a proposition for you. Big Ribs and some of the other chiefs have asked for their children to be instructed in the basics of a white education. Learning English, a little reading and writing. I would like to request that Miss—" He peered at the paper in front of him. "That Miss Montgomery take over the task while she is here. Lieutenant Liddle informs me that she is a most gifted, intelligent young woman and not likely to be frightened by the Indian children."

"I'll ask her, sir," Rand said, swallowing his dismay. The last thing he wanted was to get Sarah even more entangled in life at Fort Laramie. He kept his face impassive as the colonel outlined his plan for the school. Rand had a hard time keeping his emotions under control the last few evenings as the five of them had curled up on the floor beside the fireplace and played checkers after he and Joel had returned from their fishing expeditions. She laughed and teased like the Sarah he'd loved so long and so well. The last few evenings had been pure torture. How long must he endure her presence? He'd decided to turn his life in a new direction, and he would stick with it.

"One other thing," Colonel Maynadier said as Rand saluted and turned to go. "There's a new authorized fur trader to the Sioux downriver. Please check in on him this afternoon and see that he understands the rules governing Indian trade."

"Yes, sir." Another fur trader was the least of his worries, he fumed as he strode across the snow-covered parade ground. They were all alike anyway. All set on feathering their own nests at the expense of the Indian. They forced the Indians to pay for their own annuities with furs and made exorbitant profits when they sold the furs back east.

Sarah opened the door at his knock. Amelia was dressing in the bedroom and Jacob had already left for his duties. Sarah's eyes lit up when he repeated the colonel's request. "How lovely! It will help me feel as though I'm carrying my own weight. When does he want me to start?"

"Right away. You're to use the chapel for now, and next spring the colonel plans to build a small schoolhouse. You'll have to improvise, though. There are no schoolbooks here and probably won't be for months."

"Can I go, too?" Joel asked.

"You actually *want* to learn something?" Sarah said in surprise.

Joel looked down at the floor. "There aren't any other boys to play with. I thought maybe I could teach some of them how to play baseball."

Sarah's face softened, and she nodded. "We need to get on with your studies, too." She turned back to Rand. "Could you find me some slate? Or some paper to lay across boards?"

"There's plenty of slate in the cliffs across the river. I'll fetch some this afternoon. I have to go that direction anyway to check on a new fur trader."

ta

The sun shone coldly on the glistening snow as Rand threaded his way through the massive snowdrifts along the rocky trail that led downriver to the trader's establishment. He was cold through and through by the time he reached the group of small buildings bustling with activity. The pure snow had been tramped to a muddy quagmire by the horses tied to posts along the front of the buildings. They stood with their heads down and their backsides to the cutting gale. Sioux and Cheyenne squaws huddled out of the wind in the doorway of the storage building. He caught a glimpse of crates piled nearly to the ceiling through the open doorway. Trying to ignore the stench of so many unwashed bodies, he pushed his way into the smoke-filled room and looked around for someone in charge.

A scrawny, red-necked young man with stringy blond hair seemed to be directing the dispersal of crates. Impatience was etched around his mouth as he argued with a young Sioux brave. "We ain't dispensin' no ammunition! You savages ain't to be trusted with gunshot and powder. Here. You can have some extra bean rations."

"Must have gun powder! Need to hunt buffalo soon or squaw and papoose go hungry! Beans, bah!" The brave spat for emphasis at the young man's feet.

"Well you won't get none from me. Learn to grow crops like normal folk, and you wouldn't have to worry about shootin' buffalo. Now either take your rations and go, or get out of the way so the rest can get their grub."

The young brave scowled and swept the rations into the skirt the squaw with him held ready. He gave the young man one last angry glare before stomping away.

Rand pushed his way up to the counter, and the man looked up. Rand noticed his eyes widen, and he looked around nervously. "Captain Rand Campbell. I was ordered to see if there's anything you need. You are the new trader, aren't you?"

The young man licked his lips, and his eyes darted toward a door to the side of the counter. "No, sir. My name's Les Johnson, and I just work for him. He's in his office right now with some folks. I'll tell him you stopped by, though."

"You do that. I have another errand to run. I'll stop back later this afternoon." Rand turned to leave and almost ran into a familiar lanky figure. "Labe?" Rand stared, almost not believing his own eyes, but it was definitely Labe Croftner. What was he doing here? His blood pounded in his ears, and he swallowed the lump of rage in his throat. "Where's Ben?" He knew Labe would never roam this far from home without his brother.

"R—Rand!" Labe's eyes widened and he started to back away, but Rand grabbed his arm so tightly he flinched.

"Where is he?"

His face white, Labe shook his head, but his eyes darted to the closed door to the right of the counter. Rand released his arm and strode toward the door.

"Wait, you can't go in there!" Les moved to intercept him, but Rand brushed by him and threw open the door.

Ben was seated at a makeshift desk with two rough-looking men dressed in buckskin sitting across from him on crates. He stared at Rand, then smiled and stood. "Well, well, well, if it isn't the illustrious Captain Campbell come to pay me a call. I didn't expect word of my arrival to reach you quite this soon."

"What are you doing here, Croftner?" Rand clenched his fists and took a step toward the desk.

"What does it look like? I'm the new trader, old friend. Thanks to you I was no longer welcome around Wabash. This opportunity was too good to pass up, so I decided to put up with the disagreeable thought of having to run into you occasionally and took the job." Ben offered Rand an insolent smile and sat back down. "And a very lucrative one, too, I might add. Now if you don't mind, I have business to attend to."

Rand choked back his rage. He needed a clear head to deal with Croftner. There was some nefarious purpose to Ben's presence here, he was sure. "I'll be watching you, Croftner. You step out of line just one inch, and I'll be all over you like a wolf on a rabbit."

Ben smile indolently. "I'm terrified. Can't you see me shake?" The other men guffawed, and he leaned forward. "Give Sarah my love, and tell her I'll stop and see her real soon."

"You stay away from Sarah!"

"My, my. Does your lovely fiancée know how you still feel about Sarah? Perhaps I should inform her how you're still looking after the poor little orphan." He sat back and crossed his muddy boot over his knee. "But the beautiful Jessica doesn't have anything to worry about. Sarah belongs to me, and she's going to discover that real soon."

"You lay one finger on Sarah, and you'll be in the guardhouse so fast you won't know what happened."

"Hey, there's no law against calling on a lady."

"She doesn't want to see you." Rand wished he was as certain as he sounded.

"I think I'll just let her tell me that. I'm sure she'd be pretty cut up about discovering her precious Rand is about to marry someone else."

Tired of the exchange, Rand clenched his jaw. This wasn't getting him anywhere. "You just remember what I said." He turned and stalked out the door as the men behind him burst into raucous laughter.

His jaw tight and his chest pounding, Rand swung up into the saddle. Ranger danced a bit as if to ask what the trouble was. Rand patted his neck, then urged him down the trail back to the fort. Did Sarah know Ben would follow her out here? How much did she really care for Ben? After all, she had agreed to marry him.

When he arrived back at the fort, he marched over to see Sarah. She had her sleeves rolled up, and tendrils of hair had escaped her neat roll. He resisted an urge to wipe the smudge of flour from her cheek. "Did you know Ben is here?"

Her eyes widened. "Ben's here?" Her green eyes snapped. "He'd best leave me alone. I don't want to see him ever again."

"That's not what he says."

"You've talked to him?"

"He's a newly authorized Indian trader, and he's crooked enough to make a good one. He said to give you his love."

"The nerve of that man. I didn't have anything to do with this. You believe me, don't you?" She stared up at him anxiously.

He raked his hand through his hair. "I don't know what to believe." He started toward the door then turned back. "By the way, I got your slate."

"Don't change the subject." She caught at his arm. "You have to believe me, Rand. I didn't know Ben would follow me. I don't want to have anything to do with him."

"It's nothing to me," he said, disengaging her grasp on his arm. "I'm engaged to another woman. Remember?" He felt a small stab of guilt when he saw the look of pain cross her face.

❧

The next few days were full of getting ready for the school. By the time Monday came, Sarah felt she was ready for the new challenge. She took Joel with her as she set out for the chapel. He carried the stacks of slate for her. She didn't want him to grow up uneducated, and he was curious about the Indian children. It was a good way to interest him in studies. As she approached the small chapel, a group of about thirty youngsters watched her advance. She noticed one older girl of about fifteen. She was truly beautiful with soft, dark eyes, glossy black braids, and an eager look on her face.

The girl stepped forward as Sarah stopped in front of the door. "I am Morning Song, daughter of White Raven," she said softly. "I very glad to learn more English."

"You speak well already," Sarah smiled. "I'm very glad one of you can understand me." She opened the door and led them inside. Someone had already started a fire in the stove, and the room was warm and welcoming. She motioned for the children to be seated and waited until the rustling stopped. "I'm Sarah," she said. She didn't want them to have to start off with a difficult word like Montgomery. "Can you say Sarah?"

Dark eyes stared at her solemnly, then Morning Song spoke sharply. In unison they said, "Say-rah."

Sarah smiled. "Very good. This is my brother, Joel." Several of the youngsters had already been eyeing Joel. He smiled at them uncertainly. "Could you tell me the names of the children, Morning Song?"

The Indian girl stood and put a hand on the sleek head of each child as she spoke. "This Dark River. This Spotted Dove, this Spotted Buckskin Girl. She daughter of Chief Spotted Tail. Her Sioux name is Ah-ho-appa."

"How lovely," Sarah smiled.

The names went on and on. Sarah wondered how she'd keep them all straight. "Thank you," she said. "You'll have to help me for a few days until I can memorize them."

Morning Song nodded eagerly. "I very much like to help Say-rah."

The day went well with the children all eager to learn. Sarah was surprised how quickly they picked up the English words.

"That was fun." Joel's face shone with enthusiasm. "I even learned some Sioux."

Over the next few days Sarah was almost completely consumed with her duties as a schoolteacher. Rand seemed to be avoiding her. He rushed in for a few minutes at night, then hurried away with some lame excuse of some kind. Ah-ho-appa, Morning Song, and her brother Red Hawk came by almost every day after school. Sarah felt as though the young Indian girls were the sisters she'd always longed for. Amelia loved them, too. And Sarah was glad for Joel to have some company. He soon became best friends with Red Hawk.

Sarah and Amelia were clattering around in the kitchen and Joel was out playing with Red Hawk when the front door banged. "We're in the kitchen," Sarah called. She poured water from the wooden bucket into the kettle and set it on the stove as Rand came in. Amelia rinsed the last of the breakfast dishes and dried her hands on her voluminous apron before untying it and draping it over the back of a chair.

"Want some tea?" Sarah eyed his grim look with trepidation.

"Yeah." He pulled out a chair and sat down. "What's this I hear about you getting real friendly with some Indian kids? The whole garrison is talking about it."

"As a matter of fact Morning Song and Ah-ho-appa will be here any time. Wait till you meet them, especially Morning Song. She knows English and she's the sweetest little thing." She waved good-bye to Amelia as she patted her hair into place and hurried to meet Jacob at the sutler's store.

"I'm not sure how smart it is to let yourself get too close to them. You may be doing a lot of harm."

"Whatever do you mean? They are my friends. I would never hurt them."

"Maybe not intentionally. But have you thought about how they may become discontented with their lives as Sioux? If you give them too many different ideas, they may not fit in with their own people."

"That's ridiculous! Ah-ho-appa is a chief's daughter. Maybe she can help her people climb up out of the primitive way of life they lead." She jumped to her feet and took the steaming kettle off the stove. "You soldiers would have them stay in squalor. Rooster told Joel the only good Indian was a dead one!" She jerked her apron around her waist and tied it, before spinning around to face him.

Rand sighed and ran his brown, muscular hand through his hair. "I know a lot of the army feels that way, but you surely don't believe I do. You know White Snake was one of my best friends back home." He and the Miami brave had been friends since Rand was five. "You're new out here, Sarah. There's a lot of prejudice and bitter feelings against Indians. You need to be careful about meddling in things you don't know anything about. I wish things were different. But I've seen too many Indian women taken advantage of in the short time I've been here. I wouldn't want anything to spoil Morning Song."

Sarah opened her mouth to defend herself, but there was a timid knock on the back door. She bit back the angry words and opened the door with a bright smile. She didn't want her friends to hear their discussion and think they shouldn't come back.

Morning Song peeked in the door, and Ah-ho-appa was behind her with timid, gentle eyes. Morning Song's eyes glowed with enthusiasm and joy. Behind them Sarah heard Rand suck in his breath when he saw Morning Song's beauty.

"Say-rah, I am too early?" Morning Song dropped her eyes as Rand rose to his feet.

"I was just going. Think about what I said, Sarah." He smiled at the Indian women and strode out the door.

"You're just in time, Morning Song, Ah-ho-appa. The tea is ready." Stiff with outrage, Sarah ignored Rand's departure. He hadn't given her a chance to explain her intentions. She wanted to show God's love to her Sioux friends. She swallowed her anger and poured them all a cup of tea. Ah-ho-appa ran a gentle brown hand around the gold rim of the bone-thin china and sighed in contentment as she took an eager sip.

"What we do today, Say-rah?" Morning Song asked.

"I thought we might go for a walk while the weather holds. Some of the men are predicting more cold weather within a few days, so we should take advantage of the sunshine while we can. I thought we might walk by the river."

Morning Song nodded. Her lovely face glowed with such joy and zest for life Sarah found all her angry thoughts fading away. She untied her apron and hung it on the peg by the door, then went to fetch her bonnet and cloak from the front hall.

The wind was a gentle whisper instead of its usual gale force. Mountain chickadees chittered in the trees along the riverbank, and the sound was soothing. The last few days had been unusually warm, above freezing for a change. Morning Song skipped along beside Sarah while Ah-ho-appa eagerly led the way. They passed several groups of soldiers felling trees for firewood, the heavy thunk of their axes comfortingly familiar. For Sarah, it brought back memories of her father and brothers clearing the back pasture the summer before the war began. Those were happy days, days of laughter and contentment with Rand hurrying over every evening to take her for a buggy ride or just a walk by the river. A small sigh escaped her and Morning Song looked up, her face clouding uncertainly.

"Why Say-rah so sad? Blue coat with holes in cheeks make you unhappy?"

Sarah smiled at her friend's reference to Rand's dimples. "How did you know that?"

"Say-rah's cheeks red like apple, and she look like this when I come in." Morning Song scowled menacingly. "Eyes sparkle like dew on leaf. Say-rah love blue coat?"

Sarah nodded. "Very much. But sometimes he makes me so mad."

"Say-rah marry blue coat?" Ah-ho-appa asked.

"I want to, but first I have to convince Rand. He's being stubborn right now. I was engaged to him before the war, long before he ever met Jessica. Do you know what engaged is?"

Ah-ho-appa's sleek black head bobbed up and down. "Promised to marry. My mother wishes me to promise myself to Red Fox, but I say no. I want to marry blue coat and live in fine house like Say-rah's."

Sarah looked at her in dismay. "Oh, Ah-ho-appa, you don't mean that. It would be best for you to marry one of your own people."

"You think I not good enough for blue coat?"

"Of course not. But there are so many problems. Other people might not treat you well back in the East. And you would miss your own people."

"My friend River Flower marry blue coat and live at edge of fort. She have baby boy."

Sarah knew she referred to the common law marriages where the soldier paid the girl's father a few horses and "married" her. When he moved on to another fort, he generally left his squaw and any children behind. "You deserve more than that. Those marriages aren't legal in the sight of the white man's laws. You should look for a man who will love and take care of you always."

Ah-ho-appa shook her head, her face set with determination. "I marry blue coat or no one." She turned and started back toward the cabin with Sarah trailing behind.

Morning Song looked at Sarah sadly. "I not know Say-rah not like Sioux." She turned and walked stiffly back toward the Indian encampment.

Sarah's heart sank as she followed the girl's erect figure. What had she done? And how was she going to fix it?

eleven

Sarah was quiet that evening as they all prepared for a dance at Old Bedlam. She was worried about Morning Song and Ah-ho-appa. It certainly seemed as though Rand was right about her friends becoming discontented with their lot as Sioux because of their friendship with her. The thought of seeing Jessica with Rand only made her feel gloomier.

The place was full of smiling officers decked out in their dress uniforms, their brass buttons and black boots shining. Sarah and Amelia were claimed for dances immediately. As the awkward lieutenant whirled her around the dance floor, Sarah found her eyes straying to Rand's dark head in the throng. He was so tall, he was easy to spot. His chin rested on Jessica's gleaming red head, and she was snuggled close to him. Sarah dragged her eyes away and forced herself to make polite conversation with poor Lieutenant Richards. The evening became a blur as one officer after another claimed her for a dance. She wondered if Rand would ask her to dance, then chided herself for her foolish hope. Jessica wouldn't allow him out of her sight, she was sure. She danced twice with Isaac, Rand's bunky, and she was tempted to ask him if he knew how Rand really felt, but she resisted. It would be sure to get back to Rand and she would look pathetic.

When there were only two more dances left, Jessica's father insisted on a dance with his daughter. Rand glanced Sarah's way, then made his way determinedly through the throng.

"Are you promised for this dance?" he asked politely.

"Not really," Sarah said. "I don't think Joel will mind if he doesn't have to dance. I told him he had to dance with me so

106

he could begin to learn. But his lesson will wait." She slid into his arms, and he guided her onto the floor.

"You were right," she admitted reluctantly.

"About what?"

"Ah-ho-appa wants to marry a soldier and live in a home like mine. When I objected, she and Morning Song both thought I didn't think they were good enough to marry a white."

He nodded. "I'd heard Ah-ho-appa refused her father's choice for her. But don't beat yourself up over it. It may have happened anyway. There are a lot of Indian squaws who jump at the chance to take a soldier. And their families are well paid for them."

"That's awful!"

"I know, but it's the way things are out here. A squaw doesn't have much value. Although, as pretty as your friends are, they'll probably fetch a high price," he said regretfully. "That will be a strong incentive to their fathers."

"Isn't there anything we can do?" Sarah couldn't stand the thought of her young friends sinking into that kind of life.

"Not really. Just be a friend to them. It's probably too late to do anything else."

The dance ended, and Rand escorted her to her chair. He stared down at her with a curious look on his face. It seemed almost tender. He opened his mouth but was interrupted by Jessica's arrival.

"There you are, darling," she cooed. "Be a dear and fetch me some punch."

"Of course. Would you care for some, Sarah?"

"No, thank you," she said, turning before he could see the hurt in her eyes at his distant but polite tone.

As soon as he was out of earshot, Jessica turned to her furiously. "Just what do you think you're going to accomplish by staying here? I want you to stay away from Rand. He's mine now! You had your chance with him and you let him slip away." She stepped closer and lowered her voice threateningly. "I'm warning you, Miss Montgomery."

Sarah spread her hands placatingly. "Miss DuBois, we're just friends. And I'd like to be your friend, too."

"Then stay away from Rand!"

A spot of red on each cheek, Sarah opened her mouth to reply, but she shut it quickly when Rand returned with Jessica's punch.

Sarah was shaking as she hurried to find her cloak and go home. The party was over for her. She was tired and discouraged in spite of her bravado. Everything seemed so hopeless. Jessica was a formidable opponent.

Isaac stopped her at the door. "Leaving already?"

"I'm very tired," she said as she slipped the cloak over her shoulders.

"I was just coming to claim a dance. As compensation you must let me walk you home." Isaac grabbed his hat and greatcoat, then held open the door for her.

The cold, crisp air stung Sarah's cheeks as she took Isaac's arm on the front porch of Old Bedlam and walked across the parade ground with him. At her front door, she paused. "I'd ask you in for a cup of coffee, but it wouldn't be proper with no one else home."

He grinned. "That's all right. Maybe next time. And I really would like there to be a next time. I know you used to be engaged to Rand, but you need to get on with your life. With your permission, I'd really like to call on you."

Sarah hid her surprise. She'd seen Isaac hovering close over the past few weeks, but she had thought he was just being kind because he knew how hurt she'd been. "I don't know, Isaac," she said. "You're a good friend, and I'd hate to ruin our friendship."

"How could we ruin it? We could have some Bible study together and become better friends."

Sarah was tempted. Isaac was a good Christian man and

she had a lot of respect for him. Were things with Rand really past hope? "All right," she said uncertainly. "But I can't make any promises, Isaac."

Isaac nodded. "I understand. But we both love God, and we shouldn't shut the door on something that may be His will. Let's just see where He leads." He touched her hand briefly and turned to go.

Sarah watched as he walked back toward Old Bedlam before going inside. He was right. God wouldn't want her to marry Rand unless he became a Christian. She had to be willing to walk through any open door He chose. No matter how hard it was.

Her heart was still heavy the next morning as she and Joel set out for the school. Ah-ho-appa was conspicuously absent, and Morning Song refused to even look at her. Sarah's heart ached as she saw the stiffness in her friend's demeanor. Everything seemed such a hopeless tangle.

Things went on this way for two days when finally Sarah had enough. Thanksgiving was coming soon, and she wanted her friend to come for dinner.

"Don't go, Morning Song," she said as the Indian girl stood to go home. "I want to talk to you."

The girl almost seemed like her old self as she nodded and motioned her brother to go on without her.

"You seem to be avoiding me. I can't stand for you to be upset with me. Won't you please forgive me if I hurt you when we talked last? I really didn't mean I didn't think you were good enough for a soldier. Any man would be very lucky to get you or Ah-ho-appa. I tried to see her, but her mother refused."

Morning Song smiled. "I very angry, but no more. Say-rah my friend. I know you not wish to hurt me. And I have new friend."

Sarah's heart sank at the glow on the girl's lovely face. "A man?"

The girl nodded. "Him very handsome. Very light hair with eyes like stormy sky."

Sarah tried to think of a soldier who fit that description, but she couldn't think of who it might be. "What's his name?"

"Him new fur trader. Ben Croftner." Morning Song smiled a secret smile as she said his name.

Sarah stepped back as from a blow. "Oh, Morning Song. Not Ben. He's a very wicked, evil man." She caught the girl's arm. "Please, please stay away from him!"

Morning Song shook her hand off. "He tell me you will say this. But he loves me, Say-rah. Him good man. Give my father five horses for me. We marry tomorrow."

"Please, Morning Song. I beg you. Don't do this. It isn't a legal marriage. Ben won't stay with you."

The girl just gave her an angry stare and stalked off. "I thought my friend be happy for me, but I wrong," she called back over her shoulder. "You my friend no more, Say-rah."

Sarah clasped her hands and paced the floor. What could she do? She couldn't just stand back and let Morning Song make a mistake like that. She caught up her cloak and hurried to the door. There just might be one hope.

She borrowed a horse from the stables and found the trail leading to the trading post across the river. Jacob and Rand would both be furious if they discovered what she was doing, so she kept a sharp eye out for them as she left the fort. Luckily no one was about as she forded the river and urged the horse up the trail. It was the first time she'd been outside the fort grounds on her own. She was a little fearful and kept looking around for signs of any Indians. But she was determined to do what she had to.

The trading post was almost deserted when she arrived. A few Sioux hunkered around a fire in the front and looked up as she approached the door. Labe was just coming out the door as she slid off her horse.

"Sarah! What are you doing here?"

"I'd hoped you hadn't followed Ben out here, Labe. I need to see him. Is he here?"

He nodded. "He's in his office. I'll show you." He opened the door and led her across the dirt floor to a battered door. He rapped on it once, then swung it open for her.

Ben looked up when he heard the door open. "Sarah?" He rose to his feet eagerly, but his smile faded as soon as he saw the look on her face. His expression masked, he motioned for her to sit down on the crate across from his crude table. "To what do I owe the honor of this call?"

"I want you to leave Morning Song alone," she said abruptly. She didn't have time for any pleasantries, even if she was inclined to offer them, which she wasn't. "We both know you don't really care about her. She's too sweet for you to ruin."

He stroked his chin. "She'll be a lovely addition to my home, don't you think? And Indian women really know how to treat a man. I just don't see how I can agree with your request."

"Please, Ben. Don't do this." She leaned forward. "I can't bear to see her hurt."

"You're begging now, are you? Well, I might agree under one condition." He smiled gently. "You could take her place."

Sarah flushed. She should have known he'd suggest something like this. "You're mad. You know how I feel about you."

He stood and thrust his hands into his pockets. "You're just angry, and I'm not saying you don't have a right to be. But anything I did was only because I loved you. And you haven't had any luck with Rand, now have you?"

"Maybe not, but I couldn't marry a man I couldn't trust." Sarah stood. There was no more to say. She loved Morning Song, but it was out of her hands. Ben was the very antithesis of the kind of man God would have her marry.

"Then the wedding proceeds tomorrow as planned."

"You know it's not a real wedding! You'll just send her

back to her family when you're tired of her."

Ben sneered. "She's just a savage, Sarah. That's all Indian women are good for."

"She's sweet and good and pure. You'll take that and destroy it!"

"My, my, you do have an exalted opinion of me, don't you? Well, you just run on back to your precious Rand and let me take care of my own affairs. But don't think this is the last of our discussion. I mean to have you, Sarah. One way or the other. Things will never be over between us."

She shivered as she made her way back to Fort Laramie, and not just from the cold. Ben seemed so cold and evil. She didn't know what he might try. The fort was in an uproar when she arrived. She found Rand and Jacob mounted and ready to leave when she reached the stables.

"Where have you been?" Rand demanded angrily. "We've looked all over the garrison. You know you're never to leave the grounds unaccompanied. Rooster's predicting a blizzard. What if you'd been caught in it? What if the Sioux had taken you? Don't you have any sense?"

She slid off her horse and lifted her head. He wasn't going to browbeat her! "You don't have any say over what I do. And what would you care, anyway?" She didn't wait for his answer as she led her horse into the stable. The odor of horses, straw, and manure struck her as she escaped from the avid stares of the soldiers and the incessant wind.

Rand jumped off Ranger and followed her into the stable. "I'd care, all right!" He grabbed her arm and pulled her around to face him. "Don't you ever do anything like that again."

She stared up at him, her green eyes huge in her heart-shaped face. Did he really care, or was he just angry?

Rand muttered an exclamation and pulled her close against his chest. "I don't know what I'd do if anything ever happened to you," he whispered.

Sarah could hear his heartbeat under her ear, and she was very conscious of his warm, male scent. He stroked her hair, then pulled her away from his chest and tilted her chin up. She looked at him, her eyes luminous with tears. His eyes searched her face and he lowered his head. Sarah closed her eyes and waited for his kiss, but it never came. Rand loosened his grip on her and stepped away just a moment before Jessica came rushing into the stables. Sarah was sure her face was scarlet, and she turned away quickly to tend to her horse.

"There you are, Rand. I've been looking all over Laramie for you. I see you found Sarah. Where was she?"

Sarah's irritation rose as Jessica continued to talk as though she weren't there. "I went for a ride," she interrupted.

"A ride? Are you mad? In the dead of winter with hostile savages around? I've wondered about you before, Sarah, but this borders on lunacy." Jessica's voice was acidic. "Well, no harm done, I suppose. But you caused a dreadful commotion. It seems to me you could have thought to inform someone of your plans. Unless, of course, you wanted to upset everyone."

"I didn't mean to cause any alarm. I thought I'd be back before anyone missed me. Now, if you'll excuse me, I really must get home." Sarah brushed by her and avoided Rand's anxious gaze. She just wanted to be alone. Rand did have feelings for her, but what difference did it make? Jessica wasn't about to give him up. And Rand wouldn't be the one to break the engagement. She knew him too well. And anyway, he still wasn't a Christian, no matter how much she prayed.

The next day she watched from the window as Ben arrived with five horses to take possession of his bride. In a beautifully beaded dress bleached to a pale yellow, Morning Song was seated on a horse almost the color of her dress. Her unbound hair, rippling past her waist, gleamed in the weak sunshine as she followed her new husband back to their little cabin beside the fur post. Sarah wept as she saw her friend's glowing face look back one last time.

The next day the weather made one of its drastic changes. The temperature plummeted, and the wind picked up. Then the blizzard Rooster had predicted struck in all its fury. The wind howled and blew snow through cracks around the windows. They all had to fight to keep the fires going in the fireplace. Jacob finally gave up the fight in the bedroom and dragged the bed and their belongings out into the kitchen.

They hung blankets over the doorway into the hall to try to block the flow of cold air. By the time the storm had vented its full fury, there were drifts of snow over the windows. Jacob opened the door only to be met with a column of snow completely covering the opening. They were effectively buried until the enlisted men dug them out. It was evening before they heard the scraping of shovels and friendly hellos from outside the door.

Sarah stood beside Jacob as he opened the door and two half-frozen men stumbled inside, their faces, beards, hair, and clothing all packed with snow.

"Glad to see you all are all right," the youngest private sputtered as he complied with Sarah's urging and took off his coat before staggering toward the fire. "The colonel said to tell you to stay inside tonight. We got a path dug out pert near all around the post so we can get from building to building. And the wood detail will be here with a load soon."

The other private blew into his reddened hands, too tongue-tied at being so close to two women to speak.

Amelia poured them all a cup of hot coffee and offered them bread and jam, which they accepted with alacrity. "Much obliged, ma'am," the young private said, regretfully getting to his feet when the last crumb of bread was devoured. "We best be heading back to check with the colonel."

They saw their deliverers to the door and peered out the narrow path left by their busy shovels. "It looks like a maze," Sarah said, unable to believe what she saw. The snow towered over twelve feet in many places. The narrow path trailed down the steps and around the corner toward Old Bedlam.

Jacob saw her shivering and shut the door. "You girls had better stay in until the weather breaks. Feels like it's at least twenty below. Exposed skin freezes in seconds in this kind of temperature."

≥∙

The weather didn't break for days. There would be a couple of days of bright sunshine, but the temperatures were way below zero and the wind howled and blew the snow into ever-changing drifts. Those days would be followed by more snow and yet more snow. Sarah and Amelia took to pacing around the tiny quarters when Jacob and Rand were gone on duty. Jacob was sent out on telegraph duty several times, he was officer of the day three times, and he took his turn guarding the cattle and horse herds. They all tried to keep busy. Sarah played endless games of checkers with Joel and Amelia while Jacob and Rand saw to their duties.

Mail hadn't been able to get through either. Sarah longed for news from home. Surely Rachel had delivered the baby by now.

Jacob kept them informed of the goings-on at the post. Big Ribs had returned with the Corn band of Brule' ready to make peace. Then Man-Afraid-of-His-Horses trudged in with his band of Oglala. The winter had been hard on all of them.

Sarah was forced to discontinue the lessons with the Indian children. The weather was too cold for the little ones to be out, but she intended to start again in the spring. Her thoughts turned often to her friend, and she wondered how Ben was treating her. She continued her lessons with Joel, in spite of his protests. But no amount of activity could distract her long from her worry about her friend. And the confinement just made her dwell on the situation with Rand even more. Depression overwhelmed her all too easily.

twelve

The weather finally broke and with its usual capriciousness turned unseasonably balmy. Sarah had dreamed about Morning Song again and she was anxious about her friend; she couldn't think about anything else.

"When will you be going to the trading post again?" she asked Jacob over breakfast.

"As a matter of fact, I have to run over there this morning. The colonel has a message to deliver. Why?"

"May I come along? I want to visit Morning Song."

He hesitated, then finally gave in to her pleading eyes. "I'll have to take a couple more men along for protection. Make sure you dress warm."

She hurried to do his bidding. About an hour later, she hurried across the parade ground toward the Laramie River. Jacob and Isaac were waiting with a mount for her and five other soldiers by the ferry. She mounted and they surrounded her as Isaac led the party up the trail to the trading post.

The little settlement was full of Indians and trappers when they arrived about a half an hour later. Squaws stood around smoky fires patiently, but Sarah didn't see her friend. Isaac pointed out Ben's cabin, set off in a grove of trees by itself.

"I'll keep Ben busy," he promised.

After glancing nervously around, Sarah dismounted and hurried toward the cabin. No one answered her first knock, so she rapped harder. Finally the door opened, and Morning Song peered around the door.

"Say-rah," she gasped. She started to shut the door, but Sarah saw the marks on her face and pushed her way in.

"Oh, Morning Song," was all she could say for a moment.

The young woman's face was marred by ugly purple and yellow bruises. One eye was swollen almost shut, and her lips were split and puffy. Morning Song cried softly as Sarah took her in her arms.

Morning Song pulled away and wiped at her eyes gingerly with the hem of her apron. "Do not look at me, Say-rah. I know what you say."

"Why have you stayed?" Sarah asked gently. "Didn't you know I would take you in?"

Morning Song lifted her hands, palms upward. "Ben watch close. And he say if I leave, he make me sorry. He say he hurt Say-rah."

With an exclamation, Sarah gathered the young woman back into her arms. "Don't you worry about Ben. He can't hurt me. The blue coats won't let him." She released her. "Get your buffalo robe and any possessions you want. You're coming with me."

Morning Song looked at her doubtfully, then realized she was serious and hurried to do as her friend said. Sarah looked around curiously as her friend tied all her belongings in a sheet. The cabin was furnished with crude wooden furniture for the most part, but there were a few surprising items. One was the ornately carved and lacquered bed and the other was a silver picture frame that held a picture of Ben with his arm around Sarah. It had been taken at the county fair last summer. How cruel Ben was, she realized, to keep a picture like this in front of Morning Song.

Five minutes later Morning Song was ready. Sarah opened the door cautiously and looked around. No one seemed to be paying any attention to the little cabin set off by itself. "You stay in the trees," she told her friend. "We'll meet you just over the knoll." Morning Song nodded and slipped away soundlessly. Sarah hurried along the path and quickly mounted her horse. She told one of the soldiers to wait for Jacob while she took the others and started for home. Her heart pounded. If Ben looked out and saw her, he'd know for sure that something was up.

She looked back as she rounded the bend. There was no hue and cry, so she began to breathe easier. When she crested the knoll, she heard a scuffle and a cry to her right. "Morning Song," she called. She urged her horse through the frozen brush with the soldiers following her. As she crashed through the thicket, she saw Morning Song struggling with Labe.

"Let go of her, Labe," she ordered.

He looked up, his eyes startled. "Ben will have my hide," he whined. "I'm s'posed to see she doesn't get away. It's nothing to you, Sarah."

"Look at her, Labe. Go on. Look at her. Do you honestly think Ben has a right to beat her like that?"

Labe glanced at the Indian girl's battered face and dropped his eyes. "I told him not to, but he wouldn't listen," he murmured. "You know how Ben can be."

"I know. Now let go of her."

Labe's hand fell away, and Morning Song picked up her bundle and scurried toward Sarah. Sarah reached out a hand and helped her swing up on the back of her horse.

"Ben ain't goin' to like it," Labe said.

"I don't care what Ben likes or doesn't like. You tell him to stay away from me and Morning Song, or I swear, I'll shoot him." She nodded to the privates who had followed her, and they all crashed back through the thicket to the trail.

Isaac and the detachment were just rounding the crest of the knoll as they arrived. Isaac whistled when he saw Morning Song's face. "Ben do that?"

Sarah nodded, her lips tight. "Thanks for keeping him busy."

"No problem. We'd better hurry, though. He'll be after us any minute. He said something about going home for lunch. As soon as he sees she's missing, he's going to be hunting for her."

"He'll know where to look. Labe saw us." She quickly told him and Jacob the full story as they kicked their horses and galloped toward the safety of the fort.

When they reached the fort, Morning Song insisted on going to the Indian encampment. "I must see my father. He will wish to know," she said.

Sarah agreed reluctantly and went to her quarters to wait for her friend's return. She wasn't at all sure Morning Song's father would be able to defend her if Ben showed up.

Morning Song was barely out of sight when the front door crashed open and Ben stomped in. "Where is she?" he demanded.

Sarah rose from the chair. "Get out of here, Ben. I don't know how you have enough nerve to show your face here after what you did to Morning Song."

His face reddened. "She's just a squaw! And I can do anything I want with her. She belongs to me just like my horse! No one complains if I discipline my horse, now do they?"

"She's not a horse! And if I see you anywhere near her, I swear, I'll shoot you."

Ben laughed derisively. He strode across the floor and caught her by the arms before she could even flinch away. He took her chin in his hand and tilted her head up as she struggled to get away. "I like it when you fight me," he whispered. She stopped her struggling instantly, and he laughed again before releasing her. "Run away, little rabbit. But you won't escape me. I have plans for you."

He leered at her, then stomped back out the door. "I'll find her, Sarah. She'll wish she'd stayed where she belonged. And you'll wish you'd stayed out of it."

Sarah let out a shaky breath as the door banged behind him. How had she ever thought he was attractive and kind? She shuddered. The door burst open again, and she flinched. But it was Rand.

"Are you all right?" he asked when he saw her white face.

She nodded, close to tears. She hated to admit it, even to herself, but she was afraid of Ben. He was truly mad. "He's looking for Morning Song," she stammered, then burst into tears.

Rand crossed the room in one stride and pulled her into his arms. "It's all right, Green Eyes," he said soothingly. "We won't let him take her." He caressed her hair until the storm of weeping was past.

"I'm sorry," she gulped. "I don't cry very often. I don't know what came over me." She was very aware of his hand on her hair. That hand tightened on the back of her neck when she looked up.

She saw Rand swallow hard when she put a hand on his cheek. She searched his face and saw confusion mixed with a tenderness she'd hoped to find for weeks. "Rand," she began. But the door opened and Amelia rushed in. She'd heard the story at Suds Row.

Rand stepped away quickly, and the moment was lost. Again. Would there never be time for them to sort things out? Sarah sighed.

❧

Ben's rage was overpowering as he stomped toward the Sioux camp. He hoped the Indians would try to stop him from taking Morning Song. He would love to smash a face or two. Although the face he really wanted to destroy was Captain Rand Campbell's. As he walked in front of the officers' quarters, he heard someone call his name. Startled, he saw a lovely red-haired woman motioning to him from her front porch.

"Mr. Croftner," she called.

It must be the lovely Miss DuBois, he thought. She certainly was beautiful, if you liked the type. Cool and remote. "At your service," he said, stopping at the foot of the porch steps.

"Won't you come in, Mr. Croftner. I think we have something in common."

He raised a questioning eyebrow, but followed her inside to the elegant parlor. "And what would that something in common be?" he asked.

"We both want to keep Sarah Montgomery away from Rand," she said smoothly.

He stroked his chin. "Very true," he agreed.

"I have a plan," she said. Leaning forward, she explained her scheme, and he began to smile. It was superior in every way to his own. Sarah would learn his vengeance was terrible.

"Tell me more," he said.

❧

The next morning Sarah hurried over to the Indian camp to check on her friend, but the place was deserted. Every teepee, every pot was gone.

"They left," one soldier told her. "I think they were planning to meet up with Big Ribs."

At least Morning Song was out of Ben's clutches, Sarah thought. When she came back in the spring, perhaps her spirit will have healed from Ben's abuse. Sarah prayed so.

When she got back, Amelia and Jacob were still eating breakfast.

"What are you going to do today?" Amelia asked Jacob. Sarah sat down beside them and took a small helping of biscuits and gravy. Joel was still asleep, with only a tuft of his hair showing about the blanket.

"Wagon train's due in this morning. Rand is leading a company of us to escort it as far as the Platte River bridge and then we'll spend the night to be ready to work on the telegraph tomorrow morning. Don't expect me back until suppertime tomorrow."

"I'll miss you."

Jacob grinned and kissed her. "No, you won't. You and Sarah have all kinds of things to do. It would be a good time to start on the stenciling around the doors and windows." He got to his feet and picked up his hat. "I've got to get moving before the captain reports me." He chucked her under the chin before striding out the door.

The girls followed him out onto the porch to watch the familiar scene of guard mounting. The strains of the fort band playing drifted over to the porch, then the commander shouted, "Boots and saddles." The men swung up into their saddles in unison. The sun glittered off the men's brass buttons and weapons as they filed out of the fort. The girls watched until the troop crested the hill and was hidden from view. Sarah wished Rand would have stopped by to say good-bye. He probably said good-bye to Jessica, though, she thought, choking back tears.

≈

Rand spent the day scanning for hostiles as he plodded along on Ranger beside the slow-moving wagon train. Most of the soldiers begged to be allowed on escort duty since most wagon trains had women emigrants, but it was just another duty to him. The last thing he needed was another female to worry about; he still didn't know what he was going to do about Sarah. He couldn't shake the feeling of responsibility he still felt for her. Jessica seemed to sense his turmoil. She'd been after him to move up the wedding day to next month.

By the time they camped, Rand was bone-weary. They'd chased off a group of about fifteen Sioux, then followed them a short distance before turning back and continuing on toward their destination. At one point, Rand had one young brave in the sights of his Henry, then dropped his gun. He just couldn't do it. The youth was probably only fifteen, although he looked like he'd seen battle before—he had a livid scar running down one cheek. The brave had stared at him defiantly as Rand sighted down the barrel of his gun. When Rand let the muzzle fall, the brave lifted his spear in his hand and wheeled around with a bloodcurdling yell.

"That there was a mighty big mistake, young feller." Rooster had seen the exchange. "You'll likely run into him again, and he won't be so charitable-like."

Rooster was probably right, Rand thought as he crawled into his bedroll. But the brave had reminded him of Shane. The same careless free spirit. Rand just couldn't kill him.

❧

The weather turned frigid and stayed that way. Days went by with no relief. Finally just before Christmas, Rand informed them all they could bundle up and attend a party at Old Bedlam. The mercury had crept up to twenty degrees—almost balmy compared to where it had hovered for weeks. The Laramie Minstrels band played, and Sarah danced until she thought her feet would fall off. Isaac claimed his share of dances as well as every other officer at the fort. Several times she saw Jacob glower as Amelia swept by on the arm of yet another soldier. She knew just how he felt when she saw Rand dancing with Jessica.

Halfway through the party, a sentry rushed in. "Colonel, Spotted Tail is at the Platte!"

Colonel Maynadier jumped up. "Raise the white flag and get my horse ready." He turned to Rand. "Captain, I hate to drag you away from the festivities, but I need you to accompany me. We'll ride out to meet Spotted Tail and assure him of our good intentions. This is what I've been waiting and hoping for. He's been with Red Cloud. If Spotted Tail is ready for peace, perhaps Red Cloud is, too."

Rand nodded. "I'll meet you at the corral, sir." He pushed his way through the throng and found Sarah. "The party's over." She was pink-cheeked and breathless from a rousing round of the gallop. "I have to go," he explained.

"Not now! This is the first time we've been out of the quarters in weeks." Sarah was unable to keep the dismay and disappointment out of her voice. The break had come at just the right time, and now she felt like crying as the party broke up and everyone trailed back to their quarters.

By the time Colonel Maynadier's group of officers had

mounted, they could see the column of Brule' Sioux over the rise. The wind carried the chanting to them.

"Sounds like a death lament," the colonel said with a frown.

As they drew nearer, they could see Spotted Tail's face drawn with grief, and he dragged a travois with a shrouded body behind his horse.

A messenger rode forward and stated Spotted Tail's request. His daughter had died on the trail, and she'd begged to be buried in the white man's cemetery. Maynadier quickly agreed and Spotted Tail rode forward to talk with the colonel.

"My heart grieves at your loss, my friend," Colonel Maynadier said as the sorrowing Indian pulled up in front of him.

Tears welled up in Spotted Tail's eyes. "My heart is very sad, and I cannot talk on business; I will wait and see the counselors."

Rand and Jacob looked at one another in dread as the chief turned away. Rand had known it was Sarah's friend as soon as he saw her face.

"You tell her," Jacob said.

❧

Sarah was stitching on a lapful of quilting material in her lap when Rand strode into the parlor. The lamp light cast a soft glow over her glorious hair, and Rand caught his breath. She seemed to get lovelier all the time, he thought. He cleared his throat and she looked up.

"What is it?" She knew it was bad news by the grim set of his jaw.

He came forward and took her hand. "I don't quite know how to tell you except to just say it." He took a deep breath and taking off his hat, raked a hand through his hair. "It's Ah-ho-appa. She's dead, Sarah. Pneumonia." He cleared his throat. "It's been a hard winter, not enough food. She was too weak to fight the lung infection."

Sarah stared at him. He didn't know what he was saying. There was no way that bright life could be snuffed out.

"I'm sorry. I know you loved her."

Sarah shook her head. "There must be some mistake."

"There's no mistake. I saw her myself. Her father has asked for her to be buried in the soldier cemetery. He said she wanted to marry a soldier." His face twisted bitterly.

Sarah put her face in her hands and wept. Her smiling Ah-ho-appa. How could she be dead? "It's all my fault," she sobbed. "If she hadn't been friends with me, she would have been content with her life. She would have married some young brave who would have taken care of her."

Rand took her hands and drew her to her feet and into his arms. "I'm sorry, Green Eyes. But you did all you could for her. At least she didn't go through what Morning Song did." Rand held her until her weeping was over. "The funeral's tomorrow. I'll take you if you want."

She nodded. "I must tell her parents how much I loved her."

The next day several hundred mourners, consisting of Indians, off-duty soldiers, Colonel Maynadier, as well as Major O'Brien, who had arrived to take over command of Fort Laramie, attended the funeral.

Sarah wept as she saw the sorrowing parents and heard the story of the Indian princess who wanted to marry an army officer. It brought home to all those around that the Indians weren't some creature not quite human, but real people with emotions and pain. She knew she would never forget the grief in the mother's face.

When the funeral was over, she pushed through the crowd while Rand followed her. Tears were streaming down her face as she touched the girl's mother on the arm. The squaw looked at her with pain-shocked eyes as Sarah fumbled with a ruby pin her father gave her on her fifteenth birthday. She pressed it into the mother's hand. "I'm so sorry," she whispered.

The woman stared at her, then slowly pinned the brooch to her shawl before pulling a row of beads from her own neck and placing them around Sarah's throat. "Wash ta cola," Sarah whispered as the woman turned to go.

The Indian nodded, a weary smile flitted across her face so quickly Sarah wondered if she imagined it. Then she followed her husband, both of their heads bowed in grief.

Rand was watching her, his brown eyes warm with approval. "That was a nice thing to do. You've probably made a friend for life."

Her eyes filled again. "Ah-ho-appa was my friend. I'll never forget her. But I did tell her about Jesus, and she prayed for salvation. I can only hope she truly understood."

He nodded soberly, a little uncomfortable with her talk of religion, although he was proud of the way she'd acted. "I know it's hard for you, Green Eyes. It's all so different out here. You're used to activity and fun. It's pretty dreary confined to those small rooms all the time and never being allowed to go outside the fort. If the weather holds, how about going skating on the Laramie River tomorrow after worship services?" An army chaplain had come to Fort Laramie two days ago and they were looking forward to attending church on Sunday.

Sarah nodded eagerly. She was glad to have Rand's look of approval, but his next words spoiled it for her.

"Jessica's been wanting to go for weeks." He didn't seem to hear her quick intake of breath.

The next day was bright and sunny, with the mercury hovering near twenty-five degrees. "It feels almost balmy," Amelia said as they trooped across the parade ground to the tiny stucco chapel. Joel and Rand engaged in a snowball fight along the way and they arrived breathless and laughing.

Inside were rows of backless benches and a rough pulpit in the front of the room. It was a familiar place to Sarah, since she had used the chapel for her classes, but Amelia had never seen it and this was the first time a chaplain had been here to conduct services. Jessica motioned to Rand imperiously, and he left them to go sit with her.

Sarah drank in the words the minister spoke. She'd missed her little congregation from home so much. Until she'd come out here, she'd never realized how much the support and prayers of her friends had meant to her. A new thankfulness to God swelled up in her soul as she sang the hymns in her clear alto voice. Isaac sat beside her, and Jacob and Amelia sat on the other side. She and Isaac had enjoyed several discussions about God over the last few weeks, and she knew he was just as eager to hear the sermon as she was. She glanced over surreptitiously at Rand and Jessica. He seemed to be listening, which surprised her because he didn't seem to have much use for God since the war. And he made it pretty clear he didn't think God had a hand in the day-to-day things of life. Jessica seemed bored, though.

Sarah dragged her eyes away from Rand's broad back and fixed her eyes on the chaplain. God would take care of everything. Nothing would be allowed to happen that He didn't know about. He had brought Rand through the war safely. If He could take care of Rand physically, surely He would care for Rand spiritually as well.

Rand listened intently to the sermon. The message was a simple one of salvation through Jesus Christ alone, but it struck a chord in Rand's soul. His thoughts drifted to his grandmother, the times he had lain upstairs in the loft listening to her praying for him as she knelt by her bed in the dark. He hadn't been really happy these past few weeks. A strange discontent filled him every time Isaac talked to him about Jesus or Sarah mentioned God. They seemed so content and at peace.

He hadn't known peace since the war, but when he listened to Isaac pray, he could see the serenity in his friend's face, as though God were sitting right beside him. Did God really care about the day-to-day things? How could he know for certain?

The service was over too soon for Sarah, and she had to force herself to hurry home to change for the skating party. Jessica demanded Rand's attention the entire afternoon. Every time she looked at Rand, he was smiling at Jessica.

≥

Ah-ho-appa's death cast a pall over Christmas. Sarah could not really get into the festivities. Rand brought Jessica with him on Christmas Eve to the party at Jacob and Amelia's. She sat with a supercilious smile on her face while Jacob read the account of Christ's birth from Luke. Rand listened intently and even read a passage of Scripture himself.

Was he beginning to change? Sarah hoped so. Her eyes filled with tears as she heard again the old story. Only God had been able to keep her soul in peace through the difficult months here at Fort Laramie. She was close to giving up and trying to think about the future without Rand in it, but somehow she couldn't bring herself to let go yet—even though Isaac was sweet and would make a loving, God-fearing husband.

≥

The long, hard winter gave up without a murmur in April. The nights were still cold, but the days warmed delightfully and melted the towering mounds of snow. Sarah looked eagerly for flowers, but all she saw was blowing sand and spindly brush. But Rand promised as soon as he had a break, he would take them on a picnic up the mountain where Rooster and Isaac told him was a spot full of violets.

He had left with a detachment heading for Fort Casper. Sarah took the opportunity to try to convince herself to go back home. It was almost time for Jacob and Amelia to move on. Sarah couldn't decide what to do, but for some reason, she wasn't at peace with the idea of leaving. Once Rand was back she would decide.

thirteen

Rand rolled over on his back and looked up at the dazzling display of stars above his head. They seemed closer and brighter out here. The long days on maneuvers and the free time in the evenings left a lot of time for thinking, and he'd been thinking a lot about God. Ever since Christmas there'd been a stirring in his soul. The sermon had started it. He'd tried to talk to Jessica about it, but she had looked at him as though he were mad. "Religion is for old people," she told him. "Going to church is fine. It's where one meets the best people. But don't take it too seriously."

A powerful wash of awe swept over him now as he gazed up at the glittering sky. It seemed he'd been fighting God for so long now. All his life. But now he just wanted to quit fighting, to trust in Someone bigger than himself. A quiet awakening to God's love had crept in over the past months, an awareness of His control. God was even in control of the mess his emotions were in. Surely He would tell him what to do about Sarah.

As he lay looking up into the night sky, he tried to really pray for the first time in his life. Oh, he'd prayed in prison, but it was more of a cry for help. Not a real understanding of who God was and what He wanted from him. "God, I know You're out there," he whispered. "And I want to belong to You and Your Son. I've made a mess of my life, but it's Yours if You want it—if You can forgive me." A sense of peace flooded him at these simple words, and he fought unfamiliar tears. God had heard him, he was sure of it! He could sense His presence as he drifted off to sleep, a thousand glad songs ringing in his head.

He awoke the next morning excited, but he couldn't remember at first why he was so happy. Then he remembered, and he whistled as he packed his bedroll.

"Yer awful chipper for so early in the morning," Rooster grumbled. "Keep yer whistles to yerself."

Rand laughed and trotted off to splash cold water from the creek on his face. Wouldn't Isaac be glad! He went about his tasks all that day with a cheerful expression and a kind word for everyone. Not that he'd been a grump before, but now he had a new reason to be joyful. His spirit was contagious, and soon the soldiers were working side by side singing as they restrung the telegraph wire. They had just finished when they heard loud yells from down in the ravine to their right.

"Injuns!" Rooster grabbed his rifle and vaulted onto his horse.

There was a wild scramble as the rest of the men clambered on their mounts and followed Rooster's mad charge.

"There's only three of them," Rand muttered as he fell into line. But the rest of the Sioux were hiding. As the main force leaped out from behind bushes and rocks, the charge of cavalry faltered. Instead of three, there were at least twenty-five.

"It's a trap," Captain Brown shouted. "Retreat! Retreat!"

But Rand was in the front line, and he knew retreat would just get him an arrow in the back. He slid off his horse and flung himself down behind a boulder. He took aim and began shooting desperately, pushing away the reality of his own situation. He just wanted to see his company get safely away, then he'd worry about how to get out himself.

"Git out of there, boy," Rooster shouted, wheeling around on his horse and firing at a group of Indians crouching behind a rock. "It's better to say 'here's where he ran' than 'here's where he died'!" But Rand ignored him and Rooster swore, then galloped away, still shouting for Rand to run.

Something bit into his flesh, and Rand grabbed his shoulder. His fingers were covered with blood when he pulled his hand away. A bullet? But these Indians just seemed to have bows and arrows. He heard another shot off to his left and felt a fiery sting on his left temple, then darkness claimed him.

When he awoke he was lying beside a fire. He groaned and tried to move, but his hands and feet were bound. "So you're finally awake."

He looked up at the familiar voice. Ben Croftner? Here? Where were the Indians? He shook his head to clear it. He must still be asleep. But a hard boot in his ribs convinced him he wasn't dreaming.

"So we meet again, old friend." Ben stooped and sneered in his face. "Did you really think I'd let you get away with taking my girl? But I'm going to do worse to you, Campbell. When I get through with you, you're going to wish that bullet had killed you outright."

"How–how did you get me away from the Indians?" Rand was still confused.

Ben smiled, but the expression was a cruel one. "I paid the Indians to stage an attack. They were just Laramie loafers out for enough money to buy some liquor." He leaned forward and spat in Rand's face. "Are you ready to die, Campbell?"

"Yes. Are you?" Rand was surprised at his own calm assurance, but he *was* ready. Ever since last night.

Ben's gray eyes widened at Rand's gentle tone. "You'll pray for death before I'm through with you," he spat.

"You can't frighten me with heaven, Ben," Rand said softly.

Ben gaped at him, then stood with an angry oath. "Don't tell me you've gotten religion," he jeered. "If that doesn't beat all! Hey, Labe, Rand thinks he's going to heaven." He sneered and spat on the ground. "But he's going to find out what hell's really like before we're through."

Rand turned his head as Labe shuffled from behind a rock, fastening his suspenders. "Sorry to see you're mixed up in this, Labe," Rand said evenly.

Ben laughed again, an ugly laugh with no mirth in it. "Too bad you're mixed up with this, Labe," he mimicked. He tossed a shovel toward his younger brother. "Get digging."

Labe cast one agonized glance toward Rand's prone figure, then picked up the shovel and began to dig a small hole. He took a stake out of the knapsack beside the fire and pounded it into the hole, all the while keeping his eyes averted from Rand's gentle gaze.

Then Rand realized what Ben was planning. He was going to stake him out in the sun! A slow death, but a sure one in this deserted terrain. *Lord, help me to die with dignity,* he prayed silently. *And take care of Sarah.*

A few minutes later Labe finished his task and threw the shovel down, then wiped the sweat from his face with his shirt sleeve. "I'm done, Ben," he said with a helpless look at Rand.

"I'm not blind. Grab his feet." Ben grabbed Rand by his wounded arm and dragged him toward the two posts.

Rand clenched his teeth to keep from crying out from the pain. His face was pale beneath his tan and beads of sweat broke out on his forehead as he fought to retain consciousness.

Ben took a knife and began to cut his clothes off him. "Don't just stand there—help me, you fool," he snapped.

Labe shuffled forward and pulled off Rand's boots and socks. Ben grinned as he wound rawhide strips around Rand's wrists. "Think of me with Sarah as you're lying out here, old friend. Stage two of my plan is being put into action right now. You're little fiancée won't be too thrilled with this part of the plan, but her plan for Sarah was pure genius."

"What are you talking about?" Rand groaned as his wounded arm was wrenched above his head and bound to the stake. Sarah! What would become of her?

"Your little hussy cooked up a pretty good scheme to help me get Sarah. It's really what gave me the idea for this little rendezvous here."

"Jessica? What did she do?"

"You just stew about it while you're dying. But you can go knowing I'll take good care of Sarah."

Labe tied Rand's ankles to the stakes, then stood up dusting his hands.

"You'll never get my blood off your hands if you leave me here, Labe," Rand whispered.

"Shut up." Ben kicked him in the side, then turned to his brother. "Get our things and let's get going."

Labe's mouth worked soundlessly, and he hesitated. For an instant Rand thought he was going to defy his brother, but in the end, Labe dropped his head and shuffled off to obey Ben.

The two brothers swung onto their horses and stood looking down at Rand lying spread-eagled on the rocky ground. "So long, Rand." Ben smiled cruelly. "The best man always wins, you know. You were never ruthless enough."

Rand watched as they rode off, biting down on the pleading words struggling to escape. Wouldn't Ben love it if he begged for mercy? He turned his head away from the direct glare of the sun and began to pray for an early death.

✦

After two days with no water, the burning sun scorching every inch of his exposed skin, Rand was delirious. He muttered incoherently, sometimes shouting, sometimes screaming. The nights were bad, too. The warm spring days plunged to cold nights and Rand shuddered with the cold.

At one point he realized he was quoting the Twenty-third Psalm. "Yea, though I walk through the valley of the shadow of death, I will fear no evil." He was surprised he still remembered it after all these years. He'd learned it at his grandma's knee when he was eight. But this was the valley of the shadow of death, and somehow, he wasn't afraid to die. But something inside kept him from giving into the fever that racked his body, something stopped him from letting his spirit slip away.

The morning of the third day, he awoke relatively clear-

headed after a night of blessed coolness. His lips felt thick
and his tongue filled his mouth. Today he would probably die,
he knew. But at least he could see the land he loved with clear
eyes one last time. His eyes closed tiredly several times, but
he forced them open. This time when he fell asleep, he didn't
think he would ever awaken. But the sun began to take its
heavy toll, and he slipped into delirium for what must be the
last time. His final thought was of Sarah and he prayed for
God to watch over her.

fourteen

The next morning was a beautiful day. The girls were tired of being cooped up, and Sarah was too happy at the thought of Rand's imminent return to feel like doing any housework. She and Amelia decided to go for a stroll in the sunshine. They had barely stepped foot outside the door when Jessica hailed them.

"Sarah! Amelia!" She was dressed in a cream percale gown with cream lace lavished on it.

The girls stopped and waited as she came toward them. Sarah raised her eyebrows at Amelia. "Hello, Jessica," she said as the other girl stopped in front of them and caught her breath.

"I was hoping to find you," Jessica said. "I haven't seen much of you lately. Isaac has arranged for a detachment to escort Mother and I on a picnic. Would you like to come?"

Sarah and Amelia looked at one another. "Why?" Sarah asked. "You've made no secret of how you feel about me all winter. Why the change?"

Jessica smiled winningly. "I know, and I'm really sorry. I'd like us to be friends. Can't we start over? The fort is too small for enmity between us."

Sarah was silent a moment. There had to be some reason Jessica wasn't telling, but this might be an opportunity to get better acquainted. And she was weary of the tiny area she was allowed. It would be grand to see some new terrain. That was the one thing she hadn't accepted about fort life yet. The restrictions. Back home she was used to going for long rides by herself, wandering in the woods, or just walking along a country road. Now she was not allowed off the fort premises without a guard of at least five soldiers. And it seemed the fort's parade ground got smaller and smaller every day.

"All right," she said. "We'll go pack some food."

"Don't bother. Mother has packed enough for an entire troop." Jessica chatted easily as they strolled to the stable. Isaac had their mounts waiting for them, already saddled with sidesaddles. He helped them up, and they followed him west toward the purple mountains. A detail of twelve soldiers followed them.

Jessica kept up her smiling chatter, and gradually Sarah and Amelia relaxed. *It's just too bad she can't be like this all the time,* Sarah thought. They found a grassy area near an outcropping of rocks and spread out their blankets. The air was pungent with the scent of sage.

After lunch they decided to mount their horses and ride a bit over the rough terrain. Isaac was hoping to find some game.

Sarah let her horse pick its way up the winding trail, and breathing in the scent of sage, she reveled in the sense of well-being at being out of the confines of Fort Laramie. The men had been listening to Jessica tell a story about a ball in Boston and paid no attention as Sarah let her horse walk farther and farther away from them. Even Amelia didn't notice. At the top of the bluff, she slid down off her horse and sat down where she could look at the fort below her. She chuckled as she saw Isaac's sudden agitation when he discovered she was missing.

I suppose I should let him know I'm okay, Sarah thought. She raised a hand and opened her mouth to call to him, when she heard her horse whinny behind her. She stood quickly and turned to see an Indian brave, heavily painted, galloping toward her. She froze in sudden terror, then tried to put her foot into the stirrup and mount. But the Indian was upon her in an instant. He leaned down and scooped her up, his horse barely pausing as he caught her.

Sarah struggled to get away, gagging at the odor of bear

grease and sweat, but his arm was like a steel band around her waist. She screamed, certain she was doomed. But the crack of a rifle sounded and the Indian slumped against her and his arm loosened. She wrenched free and fell from the horse. Stunned from the swiftness of both the attack and her rescue, she lay on the hard ground as the Indian wheeled away, his face glazed with pain, holding a hand to his bloody shoulder.

Rooster galloped out of a stand of trees, his cap gone and spiky red hair standing straight on end. "What's wrong with you, gal? Don't you got no sense at all?" He slid down off his horse and pulled her to her feet. "Git on that horse now!" He shoved her up into the saddle. "There's prob'ly more of them sneakin' varmints around. We gotta git to the fort." He slapped her horse's rump, and they started down the bluff.

Isaac and Amelia, with the rest of the soldiers, met them at the bottom. Isaac's face was tight with anger. But before he could say anything, they heard a whoop behind them and turned to see a group of Indians charging toward them. "Get going!" Isaac fell back and began firing at the Indians to give Rooster time to get the girls to the safety of the fort.

Amelia and Sarah kicked their horses into a mad dash for the fort as Mrs. DuBois screamed and moved faster than Sarah had ever seen. Jessica kicked her horse into a gallop, her face calm, and the rest of the soldiers brought up the rear. Once Sarah heard a bullet whistle by her head as she clung to the horse's back. Then her horse stumbled and she catapulted into a thorny bush. Her skin was pierced in a dozen places, and she lay there too stunned to even move.

A young brave galloped up, brandishing a knife. Before she could even think to scream, he cut her loose from the thorn bush and hauled her up in front of him. Sarah tried to struggle away, but her head was throbbing from the fall, and soon darkness descended.

≈

Rand cried out and thrashed as the cooling night awoke him,

shivering as the chill breeze swept over him. He vaguely remembered a dark face swimming before his eyes off and on. Someone forcing water down his parched throat. He tried to move and found his hands and feet were unbound. He looked to his right and saw that Ranger was tied to a tree nearby. Rand sat up slowly, his head spinning. Beside him lay a skin plump with water. He took it and drank greedily, then wiped his mouth. A buffalo robe covered the lower half of his body. Puzzled, he looked around. Who had cut him free? He frowned and tried to concentrate on the dark face at the edge of his memory, but nothing more would come.

Where were Ben and Labe? He looked around slowly as his head continued to clear. The sun lay low in the sky. Only an hour or so of daylight was left. He swallowed another swig of water and shook his head to clear it, then stood to his feet. He swayed, then staggered toward his horse. A pile of soft buckskin lay at Ranger's feet. He stooped and picked up a pair of leather breeches and calico shirt. Grimacing with pain. He pulled them on over his scorched skin. They were a little loose, which helped some, but they still chafed against his throbbing skin.

Some jerky was strung over the pommel of his saddle and his mouth watered when he saw it. He stuffed some in his mouth as he leaned his head against Ranger's flank. Fortified with food and water, he forced himself to swing up into the saddle. He swayed weakly and caught at the pommel to steady himself. He had to make it. Sarah depended on it. He suddenly remembered what Ben had said about Jessica. What did Ben mean about Jessica's scheme? How could she be involved with a man like Croftner?

He urged Ranger to a trot and clung tightly to avoid slipping out of the saddle. Within an hour he was in familiar territory. Maybe he could make Fort Laramie before it was fully dark, he thought. But his horse was exhausted, and he was forced to walk. He was still weak from his ordeal, and he had to stop often to catch his breath. He stopped for the night about five miles southwest of the fort on a bluff. Barely conscious, he crawled into his bedroll and was soon fast asleep.

The next morning he awoke ravenous. His sunburn still throbbed, but he was stronger. His store of food was all gone, and his ammunition was low. But he was almost there, so he took his rifle and made his way down to the river. It wasn't long before he'd shot a jackrabbit. It was tough and stringy as he ate it hot from the spit, but it would do. At least it would give him the strength he needed to get home.

He saddled up Ranger and swung up into the saddle. In spite of the deceptive distances, he knew he'd be home soon. The fort drew nearer very quickly. Now he could make out the individual buildings. There was the commissary and the stable. The barracks and the hospital. Was he too late? He urged Ranger into a gallop.

Rand arrived about eight o'clock. There seemed to be an uncommon amount of activity going on as dozens of soldiers jostled one another in their hurry to catch a mount and saddle up. He heard Rooster, his voice shrill with emotion, calling for a fresh horse.

His heart pounding, Rand spotted Jacob and Isaac saddling horses beside the post headquarters. He kicked his mount into a canter and pulled up beside them. "What's going on?"

Jacob's voice was grim. "Indians got Sarah."

The clipped words hit Rand like a blow. Not Sarah! He felt lightheaded with shock. "When?" And he'd been worried about Ben and Jessica's plan!

"This morning. We're just back for fresh horses and supplies. You coming?"

"Let me get a fresh mount." Outwardly he was calm, but inwardly he was churning with a cauldron of emotion. Anger, guilt, love. He realized in a blinding instant what a fool he'd been. He and Sarah had something precious, and he had treated it as something of inconsequence. And now it might be too late. He shuddered at the thought of what Sarah had perhaps already endured.

He followed Isaac and Jacob out of the fort as they caught up with Rooster on his way to pick up the trail.

Just before dusk they found a spot where a large group of horses had trampled the ground. "Some of these prints belong to white men," Rand said, kneeling in the dust. "Look here, Isaac. Shod horse prints and boot heels."

"Looks like two, maybe three, men," Isaac said with a frown.

Rooster came up behind them. "Sure am glad to see you, boy. You look bad, though. Yer skin's blistered and peeling. What's happened to you? How'd you git away from them redskins?"

"I'll tell you later," Rand said. Finding Sarah was more important.

Rooster nodded. "What'd ya find, boys?" he asked kneeling beside them.

"What do you make of this, Rooster?" Rand gestured to the telltale marks. "What would white men be doing with a pack of Indians?"

Rooster studied the ground for a moment without replying. "Don't look too good, young fellers. Don't look too good at all." He stood up and scratched his red hair. "Injuns and white men. Renegades, most likely." His brown eyes were compassionate as he turned to Rand. "Looks like maybe they got Sarah."

Rand shuddered. He felt as though his whole body turned suddenly to ice. Jacob clapped a hand on his brother's shoulder. "Don't give up hope yet, Rand. We'll find her. White men move slower than Indians. We have a better chance of catching them now."

Rand nodded, but inside himself he knew Sarah was lost to him. And it was all his fault she was out there with depraved men in the wilderness far from her family and all she loved.

He felt almost mad with worry and grief as Rooster found the trail, and the detachment followed it up into the Laramie Mountains. The landscape grew more barren as loose rock over a bed of sand made travel more and more treacherous. As they rode, Rand told Rooster and Jacob about his ordeal and what Ben had said.

By the time it was too dark to follow the trail any longer, they were near the peak of the mountain. The night air was already cold, and a crisp tang to the air mingled with the scent of sage and the smoke from the fire as Rand unloaded his supplies and prepared to bed down near Jacob and Isaac.

"I'll take the first watch," Rooster said, taking his rifle out of its sling on his horse and walking over to a large boulder thrusting up through the thin soil.

Rand lay down on the hard ground and stared up at the sky, vaguely aware of the crackling fire to his right as he gazed at the bright panorama of stars above his head. The fire pushed back the blackness of the night, but nothing could push away the blackness in his soul as he thought about what Sarah might be going through right now. The plaintive howl of a pack of coyotes somewhere in the valley below him somehow added to his anguish. He prayed fervently for Sarah's safety, but he was so consumed with guilt, he couldn't keep his thoughts together. The fire died to embers before he finally slept.

❧

When Sarah awoke she found herself on a pallet on a hard, dirt-packed floor. She sat up slowly and looked around the tiny, one-room cabin. A rank odor rose from the grimy blanket over her, and she pushed it off with a shudder of disgust as she rose to get a better look at her surroundings.

Her head throbbed and the room spun around as she took a step toward the small, oilskin-covered windows. She paused until her head cleared, then moved gingerly toward the door. She raised the latch and tugged at the door, but it refused to budge no matter how hard she pulled. She leaned her throbbing head against it and burst into tears.

What am I going to do? Those savages could be back any minute, she thought wildly. She could still see the painted face of the Indian who grabbed her. But why wasn't she at an Indian camp? And whose old cabin was this anyway?

But there were no answers to her questions, so she pushed away the tears and looked around for another avenue of escape. Her body ached in a hundred places from her contact with the thorn bush, and she limped as she picked through the debris on the dirt floor.

She found a small stool among the litter of papers, old tin cans, and rags and dragged it under the window. Standing on the stool, she pulled the torn oilcloth away from the window and tried to pull herself through.

But the tiny opening was much too small for even Sarah's slim shoulders, and the stool collapsed under her weight, one leg rolling useless across the floor, as she fell to the ground. She gave in to helpless tears again. *What am I going to do, Lord?* she prayed. She was hungry and thirsty and scared. Judging by the light, it was close to noon, so she must have been unconscious nearly twenty-four hours. It was no wonder her mouth was like cotton, she thought when she finally calmed down.

She sat there until the sun no longer shone through the east window, feeling more and more abandoned. What if she was left there to die with no food or water? Panic at the thought overwhelmed her, and she ran to the door and pounded on it. She heard the sound of horses, then the click of a lock being pulled back on the other side of the door.

Trembling, she rose to her feet and faced the door, so frightened she felt faint. *Help me, Lord,* she prayed as the door swung open.

The sudden flood of sunlight into the dark cabin blinded her momentarily, then she blinked in surprise as she recognized the two figures framed in the doorway.

"Be—Ben?" she croaked through her parched throat.

"You don't look too good, love." Ben grinned as he saw her torn and stained dress; her hair, tangled and matted, hung down her back and dirt smudged her frightened face.

Although she would rather anyone else rescue her, Ben was a welcome surprise from the savages she'd expected. She had opened her mouth to thank him when she noticed how unsurprised he seemed to see her.

"Been awake long?" he asked.

"You knew I was here?" Her voice was halting and incredulous.

"Of course." He kicked some refuse away from the door. "Shut the door, Labe." He reached out and touched a lock of her hair, and she flinched away. His lips tightened as he dropped his hand. "The Indians were eager for the guns I offered for the 'soldier girl with hair like the sun.' But I must give credit where credit's due. Jessica came up with the idea."

Sarah felt the blood drain from her face. Ben and Jessica had arranged for her kidnapping? But why? Her lips quivered as she forced back tears of weakness. She didn't want to give him the satisfaction of seeing her cry.

"Aren't you interested in why you're here?" The cruel light in Ben's eyes grew as he saw how her green eyes dilated with terror. "Well, let me tell you what I have planned. Remember that marriage we were supposed to have? You should have been my wife by now. Well, I aim to put that to rights." He pulled her to him and wrapped a hand in her hair.

A moan escaped Sarah's tight lips as he pulled her hair even tighter. "Too bad about your beloved Rand," he sneered.

A shudder shook Sarah's frame, and she closed her eyes. "Wha—what do you mean?"

"Just that your precious Rand is dead by now." He smiled unpleasantly.

Rand dead? She wouldn't believe it. After all, she'd believed Ben before—and look what had happened. She opened her eyes and stared into Ben's face. How had she ever considered marrying him?

The silence grew heavy as Ben stared back at her. Labe's nervous shuffle broke the silence. Sarah turned her eyes toward him. "Please," she whispered. "Please, Labe, help me."

Labe's eyes darted from his brother's set face to Sarah's white one. "Come on, Ben. Let's take her back. She won't say nothin', will you, Sarah?"

"No. No, of course not." Sarah wet her dry lips with the tip of her tongue. "Just take me back to the fort, and I'll say you rescued me from the Indians. You'll be heroes."

Ben's lip curled in disgust. "You must take me for a fool!" He let go of Sarah's hair and shoved her off her feet, then spun toward Labe. "Get out!" He pushed his brother toward the door.

"Help me, Jesus," Sarah said under her breath. While Ben's back was turned, her hand groped along the dirty floor; her seeking fingers closed around the broken stool leg. As Ben bent over her, his hand gripping her shoulder, she twisted around and with one last desperate effort, she smashed the stool leg against his head. He slumped against her without a sound.

Scrambling to her feet, she rushed to the door and pulled it open. She blinked as she surveyed her surroundings. The tiny cabin was in a small clearing surrounded by heavy forest. A meadow filled with wild flowers was in front of the door, and a narrow, barely discernible path ran through the middle of the meadow. She caught a glimpse of Labe's head over near a stand of aspen.

Watching to make sure Labe didn't see her, she stumbled along the path, casting furtive glances behind her to make sure neither Labe nor Ben was following her. The path narrowed further, then disappeared at the bank of a small stream. Sarah sank to her knees and drank.

Birds twittered from the budding branches above her head,

but that was the only sound as she followed the stream into the forest. The stream soon joined a larger river, and Sarah hurried along the bank. She wondered how long it would be before Ben regained consciousness. He would pursue her, she knew; she had to get as far away as she could.

&

Labe had fallen asleep leaning against an aspen tree, but he woke with a jump when Ben staggered out of the cabin. "Where is she?" Ben looked around wildly.

"Who?" Labe peered past Ben into the dark cabin, expecting to see Sarah inside.

"Who do you think?" Ben held his aching head and tried to think. "Why didn't you stop her?"

Labe finally grasped that Sarah had escaped—and that Ben was blaming him. "Honest, Ben, I didn't see nothin'." He backed away from his brother's furious face and stared slack-jawed as Ben stumbled toward the horses. "What are you doin'? I thought we was going to hole up here for a few days."

"Plans have changed." Ben tightened the cinch on his mare's belly. "Thanks to you, I've got to track Miss Sarah down."

"Can't we just leave her be?"

Ben wiped away a bit of blood from his face. "She's not getting off after what she did to me." He swung into the saddle and waited impatiently while Labe followed suit. Ben's face was hard with anger. No one got in Ben Croftner's way without paying for it.

&

When the sun told her it was midafternoon, Sarah stopped beside the river. Her head was light from lack of food, and she had to rest for a moment. She sank down to rest on a large rock and looked around, trying to think. She had to find something to eat, she realized, or she'd never make it. Wearily, she forced herself to her feet again and began searching the bushes, grateful for the forest lore Rand had taught her when they were growing up. After several minutes, she found some berries she knew were edible, despite their bitter taste, and she crammed handfuls into her mouth, grimacing at the flavor. Using her fingernails, she dug the roots of another edible plant out of the ground. She washed the soil off in the river and then crunched them down.

A little clearer headed, she stared along the riverbank again. She would make it, she told herself. God was with her, no matter where she was. With His help, she would find her way back to her family.

But by the next morning, she was no longer so certain. The mosquitoes had swarmed around her all night, a living haze of biting misery. She was weak now from hunger and fatigue, and the night's noises had driven her nearly mad with fear. Coyotes had howled, their voices closer than she had ever heard them, and once a large animal had snuffled right next to her, causing her to freeze, too terrified to move for several long minutes.

Now, as the sun rose in the sky, her steps were slow and dragging. She rounded a curve in the river, forcing herself forward, and then stood still.

She was face to face with a band of ten or so Sioux braves. Their faces were painted and one young brave had a livid scar across his cheek. The blood drained from her face, and then darkness claimed her.

fifteen

The men rode silently through the woods, hardly looking at each other for fear they'd see the foreboding in one another's eyes. Jacob reined his horse in suddenly and dismounted. He bent over and picked something off the ground.

"What is it?" Rand's voice was hoarse. He held out his hand and Jacob dropped a brooch into it.

They'd both seen it many times. The delicate filigree rose customarily adorned the bodice of Sarah's dress. Rand had given it to her for her birthday the year he left for the war. He stared at the dainty pin, and his face turned hard as he fought to control the pain that surged through him. "At least we know we're on the right trail," he managed to say at last. He tried to smile, but it looked more like a grimace of pain. "Everyone always said Rooster could follow a wood tick on solid rock." He picked up the reins, gripped by a renewed sense of urgency. "Let's get going."

Rooster led the way, his keen eyes following the fresh trail. They splashed across the stream and picked their way up a steep hill. Rooster glanced around at the silent men as they paused at the top of the hill. "Reckon we all fell a little bit in love with that gal," he said morosely.

"Don't say it like she's gone!" Isaac's knuckles were white where they gripped the reins. "We can't be more than a few hours behind her." He urged his horse forward and took the lead through a line of trees.

Rand and Jacob, following close behind, reined in at the sound of a startled snort. Two bear cubs bleated and rolled toward their mother. She swung around from her perusal of a fallen tree trunk, ready to face the threat to her offspring.

Rand's eyes met the grizzly's, and he read the rage there. She roared angrily as she rose to her hind feet, a good seven feet tall. Her mouth wide with another roar, she dropped to all fours and charged toward them.

Jacob was closest, and his horse shied. Caught off guard, he fell to the ground. He stared up at the saliva dripping from the bear's giant mouth, and then he grabbed for his gun, but it had fallen from his holster when he catapulted from the saddle. He scrabbled backward, away from the grizzly.

"Lay still, boy!" Rooster said softly. He aimed his Winchester at the bear's head, just as Rand frantically aimed his own gun. The rifles barked, but not before the grizzly swiped at Jacob's leg with her evil claws. She swung her head in dull surprise, then crashed to the ground beside Jacob.

Blood was already pouring from Jacob's leg, soaking his torn pants. "Quick, hand me the canteen," Rand shouted, kneeling beside his brother.

Rooster handed him the canteen. "Clean it good, boy, or it'll fester for sure. No telling where that bear's claws have been."

Rand ripped the fabric away from the wound and splashed it with water again and again. Jacob's flesh was flayed so badly that the bone gleamed through the shredded skin. Rand tried to keep the dismay from his face as he bound the wound with a clean handkerchief.

Jacob's face was pale and sweat sheened his forehead as he gritted his teeth against the pain. "Sorry, Rand." His face contracted in pain and frustration. "We were so close."

Rand patted his brother's leg. Isaac crouched beside him and gave Jacob a sip of water. "How bad is it?" he asked Rand softly.

"Bad." Rand shook his head and turned away so Jacob wouldn't hear. "It's deep in his thigh muscle—to the bone. He'll be in even more pain when the shock wears off. We need to find someplace for him to hole up." He paused bleakly. "He won't be riding for a while."

Isaac nodded. "I hunted this area last year. If I remember right, there's a small cabin just beyond the woods to our north. Let's make for there. It's almost dark anyway."

Rand fought to keep the despair from his face as they made a rough travois to carry Jacob. This delay could be deadly for Sarah.

Isaac led the way through the trees. Rand spared a thought for the motherless bear cubs, but he knew there was nothing they could do for them. He found himself smiling, thinking that if Sarah were there, she would probably have insisted they catch the cubs and bring them with them to raise. His smile faded, turning to a frown of pain, as he was washed anew with fear for Sarah.

The light was murky by the time they stepped out of the forest and into a small meadow clearing. The cabin squatted against the sloping north side, and they hurried toward its meager haven.

The open door creaked in the gentle breeze as they swung down off their horses. "Me and the men will take care of the horses," Rooster said. "Git that boy inside. Better clean the wound again, too."

Rand and Isaac carefully lifted Jacob off the travois and carried him into the dark cabin. "Light a lantern, Isaac," Rand said as they lay Jacob on a moldy mattress in the corner. Rand eased his brother's boots off and began to untie the handkerchief on Jacob's leg. Isaac lit the lantern, and the dim glow pushed the shadows back.

The wound had reopened from the jostling on the travois, and Jacob lay senseless. One of the other men came in with a small flask in his hand. "Rooster says he brought it along for medicinal purposes."

Rand uncapped the flask and poured a generous amount into Jacob's gaping wound. Jacob thrashed and cried out, then lapsed back into unconsciousness as Rand rebound the wound.

"I reckon that's all we can do," he said to Isaac.

"Except pray."

Rand looked at Isaac, then back at his brother. He nodded and knelt on the floor, Isaac beside him as they each asked God for His help. After a few minutes, Isaac got to his feet, but Rand stayed where he was. *Help me find Sarah, Lord. And once I do, please take things into Your own hands and clean up the mess I've made. I've been so selfish, following my own way. Please guide us now and show us what to do. Take care of Jacob, and heal his leg. And take care of Sarah. You know where she is, and only You can lead us to her.*

At last he stood up, a new peace filled his heart. He felt his first real sense of hope that they might find Sarah alive and well.

They made up their beds on the dirt floor of the cabin. Rand checked on Jacob several times throughout the night, as his brother thrashed restlessly. Finally at dawn, he touched Jacob's forehead and found it cool. He breathed a sigh of relief as he pulled on his boots and woke the others.

They were eating a cold breakfast of hardtack and dried meat, when Rooster burst into the cabin. "She was here! Our leetle gal was here!"

"What are you talking about?" Rand jumped up and gripped Rooster's arm.

"Our Sarah was here. Look!" He held out a scrap of familiar green and yellow calico.

"Where did you find it?" Rand's voice was hoarse with excitement.

"Down by the stream. And I found her trail—she's alone!" Rooster almost danced in jubilation.

Rand smoothed the scrap of fabric, almost giddy with relief. She'd gotten away from whoever had held her captive. God was working! "Let's check Jacob," Rand said, impatient to be on their way.

Jacob was sitting up, sipping a thin gruel made of water

and hardtack. He gave them a wan smile. "Sorry, Rand. Guess I won't be in any shape to travel for a few days."

Rand nodded. "I'm just thankful you're alive, Brother." He grinned, anxious to wipe the look of guilt off Jacob's face. "I have to wonder, though, if you didn't get in that bear's way just so you'd have a good story to tell back at Bedlam."

He waited until Jacob smiled weakly, and then he turned to the group of privates who were leaning against the cabin. "I want you soldiers to stay with Jacob until he can travel, then get him back to the fort. Isaac and Rooster will come with me to find Sarah." He cocked an eyebrow at his two friends. "Okay with you?"

"Let's get going," Isaac said.

Rooster nodded. "I'll saddle up the horses."

Fifteen minutes later, Rand was almost jubilant as they followed Sarah's clear trail. "That gal will never make an Injun," Rooster muttered. "She leaves a path even a greenhorn could follow."

Rand grinned in agreement. *Thank You, Lord,* he prayed silently.

Near noon, they rounded a bend in the river they were following, and Rooster stopped short. He whistled in dismay. Sarah's clear tracks were obliterated by unshod pony tracks and moccasin prints. "Bad news, fellows. Looks like the Injuns caught her."

Rand stood staring at the telltale marks, his heart pounding. So close to finding her, and now this! He swallowed hard as he fought to hold onto his new faith and hope. "Can you tell what kind of Indians?"

"Hard to say, but I'd guess Sioux."

They followed the trail for the rest of the afternoon. Rand struggled to pray, but despair kept rearing its head, coming between him and his sense of God's presence. *Dear Lord, please take care of her.*

sixteen

The band of Sioux gave Sarah jerky and fresh water before jabbering and pulling her to her feet. In spite of her terror, she was grateful for the food. She'd never been so hungry in her life. The jerky was tough, but she didn't know when anything had tasted so good.

The young brave with the scar on his face pulled her up behind him on his pony, and the entire band began to pick its way along a faint trail through the forest. Sarah would never have recognized it as a trail, but once they had followed it for a while she was able to see the slight impression from other Indian ponies. Twilight was sending out long golden shadows by the time they turned the crest of a hill and saw campfires and teepee shapes below them in the valley beside a stream.

Children jabbered and squaws stared at her with hostile eyes as the braves paraded through the camp, raising their bows and spears in triumphant shrieks. Sarah fought unconsciousness as she tried not to droop wearily against the young brave's back. Her vision blurred and doubled as the brave stopped beside a teepee and slid to the ground. He pulled her down, and she fought his grip on her arms.

"Let go of me."

He grinned at the tired anger in her voice, then thrust her inside the teepee and closed the flap, encasing her in darkness. She was too weary to do more than stumble wearily to a soft pile of furs and sink into instant sleep.

When Sarah awoke, she was in a dark, cool place. Strange chanting filled her head, and she heard the rumbles of unfamiliar voices. But the words were all jumbled together, and nothing made any sense. She tried to rise and was surprised to find she could move her hands and feet. She had thought the Indians would tie her up so she couldn't escape in the night. The sounds outside were distant and not threatening, so she snuggled back down in the furs and fell asleep again.

The next time she awoke, she was not alone. A beautiful Indian girl knelt beside her and offered her a bowl of stew that smelled wonderful. She took it and began to eat eagerly. It was flavored with unfamiliar herbs, but the meat and vegetables were tasty, and she ate it quickly. The young squaw smiled, then quickly stepped outside and closed the flap on the teepee behind her.

Sarah's shoulder protested as she got to her feet. Swaying weakly, she started toward the flap in the teepee, then staggered and sank back onto the ground. She was just too tired, she realized, to push herself any longer. She sat back down on the bearskin rug to await further developments.

While she was waiting, she looked around curiously. She'd always wondered what a teepee looked like inside, but she'd never been in one. Not even Morning Song's.

The teepee was large, at least ten feet in diameter. In the center was a tripod arrangement that supported a pot over what were now stone cold ashes, although a pile of buffalo chips lay heaped to the side. Spears and knives hung from the lodge poles, and buffalo robes were piled to one side. Pelts of various animals, beaver, wolverine, raccoon, and antelope, were in various stages of tanning on a rack of some kind.

She dragged her eyes away from the furnishings of the lodge as the flap opened and the Indian brave came in. There was a fierce scowl on his young face, and Sarah's heart pounded in trepidation. It was the youth with the terrible scar on his cheek she'd seen before. "He–hello," she stammered. Then she smiled as she remembered the Sioux Isaac had taught her. "Wash ta cola," she stammered hopefully.

The brave merely grunted, his black eyes roaming over

Sarah's bright, tangled hair. He reached out and touched a bright lock.

She forced herself not to flinch away. "Sarah." She gestured at herself. "My name is Sarah."

The brave nodded in sudden comprehension, a smile of delight winking across his face so quickly Sarah thought she'd imagined it.

The flap lifted again as the young Sioux maiden entered. She reminded Sarah of a young antelope, all long limbs yet curiously graceful. Sarah's heart clenched as she thought of Morning Song.

"You awake," she said, her dark eyes liquid with a hidden smile.

"You speak English." Sarah smiled in relief.

"Little. Little English. Live at mission one year." The girl squatted and offered her another bowl of stew. "You eat."

She wasn't really hungry any longer, but since she intended to escape at the first opportunity, she knew she needed to build up her strength as quickly as possible.

The brave grunted again and said something to the girl. "Little Wolverine say you belong to blue coat with eyes like eagle. Soldier not kill Little Wolverine in battle. Why?"

Sarah searched her memory, but she couldn't remember Rand mentioning an incident like he described. "I don't know," she admitted reluctantly.

The girl translated to the young Indian and he fired a volley of words back at her. "He say blue coat with eagle eyes spare Little Wolverine. Little Wolverine save you." She pretended to weigh her hands until they were on an equal level.

"Yes. Even. Thank you." Sarah looked into the dark eyes beside her and thanked God for sending such an unlikely rescuer. They weren't going to hurt her.

❧

Sarah's strength grew daily on the good food White Beaver, the Indian girl, brought. White Beaver gave her a beautifully beaded Indian dress to replace her torn dress and braided her hair. She looked like a beautiful red-gold Indian.

She and the young maiden grew to be friends—she felt an almost uncanny sense of friendship and identification with her as if she'd known her all their lives—and by the third day Sarah felt at home in the busy Sioux camp. The children were curious about her and soon lost their shyness when she appeared. White Beaver was happy to translate their innumerable questions.

But Sarah grew more anxious daily. Where was Rand? Was he all right? Was there any truth to what Ben told her? Could he really be dead—or did he think she was dead? Was he looking for her? She was filled with trepidation as she thought of having to explain that Ben had taken her and what his intentions had been. What if Rand blamed her? What if he thought she'd encouraged Ben to follow her out here?

"Why you so sad?" White Beaver asked as they waded in the stream fishing just after dawn on the fourth day.

Sarah's eyes filled with tears as she clambered out of the water and sat on a large rock, White Beaver following close behind her. "I miss my friends," she said simply. "And I worry about the bad man who tried to hurt me. He may be looking for me still."

White Beaver nodded slowly, her dark eyes compassionate. "Little Wolverine take you back soon. Then debt to blue coat is paid. And Little Wolverine say Sarah cry no more. He know man who hurt Sarah. He make sure he not hurt Sarah again." She reached over and touched Sarah's arm shyly. "White Beaver miss Sarah."

"I'll miss you, too," she said hoarsely. "Thank Little Wolverine for me. You are both good friends." Just a few days with the Indians had shown her how alike they all were. And she felt so sad knowing their way of life would soon be no more. She knew Little Wolverine and the other braves had no idea how many settlers were clamoring to take away the Indian hunting grounds. And Rand might actually have to fight Little Wolverine some day. She couldn't stand the thought of the bright young brave lying dead on a field of battle.

She picked up her string of fish and followed White Beaver back to camp. Why was life never simple?

ช่

Rand and his companions followed the trail as it led on through rocky hills and sagebrush-choked gullies. When they ran low on rations, Rand and Isaac brought down an antelope and cut it into jerky, smoking it overnight over a low fire. Rand alternated between worry for Sarah and concern for Jacob back at the cabin.

Four days from the fort, they awoke to a leaden sky with a stiff, moisture-laden breeze whipping across the stark landscape. Desperation clouded all three of their faces. If it rained, the trail would be washed away. And they were so close! They hurriedly saddled up and rode out.

But their haste was useless. The storm struck with its usual force in the mountains. Hail rained down on them, and they were forced to take shelter under an overhanging cliff wall. Then the thunder boomed around them as torrents of rain fell and lightning crackled overhead.

"We've got to git to high ground!" Rooster shouted above the crashing thunder. "This here's a real gully washer. There's liable to be a flash flood any time!"

Staying as close to the rock wall as possible, they led their horses up the rocky hill. Halfway up the side of the slope, Rand looked down and saw a mountain of water sweep away the tangle of sagebrush and aspen in the gully where they'd been only minutes before.

"This here's prob'ly high enough," Rooster said, pausing under an overhang.

They crouched there, hugging the side of the rocky wall. The horses shifted restlessly, but the men managed to hang onto the reins.

Finally it was over. Steamy mist shimmered in the heat as the sun broke through the clouds, and they emerged from their sanctuary. Rand was appalled at the changed landscape. The flash flood had carved new gullies and filled in old low spots, as the raging water carried away everything in its path. He stood surveying the damage, as dawning dismay swept over him. The trail to Sarah would never have survived such rain.

Rooster saw his consternation. "Don't take on so, boy. We ain't done by a long shot."

"What do you mean? How will we ever find her now?"

"I've scouted these parts before. Over yonder peak is one of the Injuns' favorite camping grounds. We'll just mosey on over there, and maybe we'll find your Sarah."

Galvanized, Rand leaped astride his horse as Rooster led the way and Isaac brought up the rear. By nightfall they were in a line of trees overlooking an Indian campground. The teepees glowed with color from the sunset. They caught glimpses of dimly illuminated figures moving around the campfires.

"Now what?" Rand asked.

"Now we stay put till later when they're sleepin'." The old Indian fighter took off his hat and smoothed his red hair. "Then we sneak in and look around for your Miss Sarah."

They tied their horses to a tree and hunkered down to wait. Rand kept watch while the other two tried to catch a little sleep. He was just about to wake Isaac for his turn at watch when he noticed a movement just below their lookout. He cocked his rifle and the other two were awake in an instant.

"What is it?" Isaac whispered.

"Don't know. Thought I saw something." Rand searched the spot where he thought he'd seen the movement. But he froze when he heard a sound on the slope above them. He swiveled his head and faced a row of fiercely painted Indians holding spears, all pointed at him and his friends.

They were obviously outnumbered, so when one of the Indians motioned for them to drop their guns, they obeyed.

The Sioux bound their hands with brutal efficiency, then marched them down the slope to the camp. They thrust them roughly into a large teepee and fastened the flap firmly behind them. Rand could see the outline of a guard through the teepee's buckskin.

The three men looked at one another with grim faces. Some rescuers they were. Now they were all in the same uncomfortable spot with Sarah, if she were even here. "Why didn't they kill us outright?" Rand asked.

"They're probably saving us for some special ceremony," Isaac said, sitting down on a buffalo robe. "We'd best get some sleep. They'll be on their guard tonight, but maybe tomorrow we can find a way to escape."

They sat down and tried to relax, but they were all too tense about what their fate would be to rest very well.

Rand sat up just before dawn, too keyed up to lie down any longer. He sat listening to the sounds of the Indian camp beginning to stir around him. He understood none of the guttural language outside as he heard squaws light fires and call to one another.

Diffused light gradually lifted the darkness inside their teepee as the bustle outside increased. Finally the flap lifted, and a young Indian brave stepped through, followed by an Indian girl. Rand immediately recognized him as the brave he had spared in the battle the week before. And he was the one whose face he'd seen in his delirium!

"I told you you'd be sorry." Rooster recognized the brave, too.

But Rand felt no fear as he looked into the youth's calm, dark eyes. Then the Indian girl stepped forward and smiled at him. "Do not fear. Little Wolverine your friend. But he say, 'Why you not shoot him?'"

Rand hesitated. His reasons would probably sound silly, but there was no help for it. "Little Wolverine reminded me of my younger brother. You know the word *brother?*"

The girl nodded. "One who shares mother and father?"

Rand nodded. "I have a younger brother about the same age as Little Wolverine. I saw that same brave spirit in Little Wolverine."

The girl smiled as she translated. The youth's black eyes never left Rand's face as she explained. Then he nodded and barked an order to the girl. She gave Rand a slight smile, then slipped out the flap of the teepee. Moments later Sarah stepped through the flap behind the Indian girl.

"Sarah!"

Sarah's green eyes widened and she gasped as Rand shouted her name and started toward her. "Rand?" She ran into his open arms, and over his shoulder she saw Rooster and Isaac beaming at her. Rand had found her! He must have been searching all this time. Joy exploded in her breast as she buried her face against the rough wool of his uniform.

"Who did this to you?" He frowned as he looked at her bruised and battered face. "And how'd you get away from the renegades who had you?"

"I–I came to a cabin," she stammered. She flushed at Rooster's gaze, his curly red eyebrows cocked questioningly, but she wanted to talk to Rand about Ben when they were alone. "Later," she whispered to Rand. She turned to the two Sioux standing silent behind her. "I would have died if it weren't for my friends. I'd like you to meet Little Wolverine and White Beaver."

Rand held out his hand to the two Sioux. "I don't know what to say—how to thank you."

The girl smiled. "Sarah and Sioux friends. We miss her. You leave in morning for soldier fort but first we have feast."

Rand could sense the good will coming from the two before him and he thanked God in his heart for working all things out for good just as He'd promised. It was almost too much to take in that his impulsive act of mercy could have such far-reaching consequences.

Rooster and Isaac crowded close and hugged Sarah. She couldn't help the tears of joy that trickled down her cheeks.

They spent the day with their new friends. Sarah insisted on smearing a foul-smelling ointment White Beaver had given her on Rand's peeling skin. It soothed his sore and itchy burn amazingly well. As they sat beside the stream and talked, Rand told her about his salvation and she wept tears of joy that God had answered her prayers.

As some of the women prepared a feast for the evening, others were kept busy taking down teepees and preparing to move camp. "What's going on?" Rand asked White Beaver. The girl drew him off to one side. "We go to make war with Red Cloud at Powder River."

Rand's face mirrored his shock. "Don't go, Little Wolverine. I don't want anything to happen to you. Tell him not to go," he appealed to White Beaver.

The Sioux brave drew himself up straight and taut as the Indian girl translated. "He say, 'Should Little Wolverine stay in camp like dog and let others fight for his family? Soon people have no hunting grounds. Whites take all. Red Cloud say Indians must fight or be forced to farm.' "

The brave spat in the dust. "He say, 'Braves not dirt diggers.' " Little Wolverine's face softened as he spoke again and White Beaver continued to translate. "But he say, 'Rand and Little Wolverine, brothers. They not fight.' "

"No, my brother." Rand laid a hand on Little Wolverine's shoulder. "We'll not fight. And someday I hope we meet again."

The brave clasped his hand over Rand's large, square hand on his shoulder as though he understood his words before White Beaver translated them. His dark eyes were warm with friendship.

Rand wasn't sure how the bond between them had come to be, but it was there as surely as the one between his real brothers, and he'd known it as soon as he looked into the

Indian's eyes at their first confrontation. "May God keep you safe, my brother," he said.

The next morning they said their good-byes to their new friends as soon as dawn broke.

seventeen

Amelia watched the hills surrounding the fort every day, anxious for word of Sarah. The main detachment had returned, hauling Jacob home two days ago, but no one had heard a word from the three who pushed on after Sarah.

After breakfast on the third day of Jacob's return, Amelia sat on the porch railing, watching as the cavalry prepared for maneuvers. Joel sat listlessly beside her. "Boots and saddles." Captain Brown shouted the familiar command to mount and the cavalry swung up on their horses and rode out of the fort.

Jacob limped across the parade ground to join her in her vigil. "The commander says there is still no word. They haven't shown up at Fort Casper or the Platte River Bridge Station."

Amelia burst into tears and buried her face against Jacob's chest. "I have a terrible feeling she's dead," she sobbed. "And we'll never know for sure."

Jacob patted and soothed as best he could. Joel stood up suddenly and pointed west. "What's that?"

Jacob turned and looked, then grew suddenly still, his eyes scanning the slope to the west of the fort. He pulled Amelia away. "Wait here."

"What is it?" she protested as he took off in a running limp for the stable. But then she saw four riders coming down the rocky incline toward the fort. And one of them, dressed in buckskin like a squaw, had sunny red-gold hair. With a sob of relief, she picked up her skirts and ran after Jacob.

"They've got her!" a sentry to the west of the fort shouted as soldiers ran from the mess hall and barracks to greet their beloved Sarah. Amelia wasn't the only one who had just about given up hope.

Soldiers lined the road and cheered as the four travelers, tired and dusty, rode into the fort.

"Sarah!"

With a sob of joy, Sarah slipped off her mare and fell into Amelia's arms. Laughing and crying, she hugged Amelia then Joel as soldiers cheered and whistled and slapped each other on the back in jubilation. Even the post commander was out to greet them.

Joel clung to her as Amelia led her home. She heard Rand laughing as he tried to tell their story. But the true story still had to be told.

Amelia sent Joel out with the men, then heated a kettle of water and poured it into a hip bath as Sarah peeled off the dusty, stained buckskin dress. She poured cold water into the bath and tested to make sure it wasn't too hot, then as Sarah eased in with a sigh, she began to comb the tangles out of her friend's red-gold locks.

A half-hour later, hair washed and clad in clean clothes, Sarah curled up on the sofa while Amelia stood over her, plaiting Sarah's hair into a long braid. "You have so many bruises. But of course the Indians are notorious for their brutality." She'd been appalled at the dozens of bruises on Sarah's body.

Her friend's sympathetic touch and voice broke the dam on Sarah's emotions and she burst into tears. She had to tell someone—she couldn't hold it inside any longer. "It wasn't the Indians, Amelia—they helped me. It was Ben!"

Amelia's fingers in Sarah's hair stilled. "Ben Croftner? He beat you?" Her voice was incredulous. She detested Ben, but he had always seemed a perfect gentleman, courteous and gentle.

In a flood, the horror of her ordeal gushed out. Amelia sat and held her as sobs ravaged her body and she choked out the truth.

"Did you tell Rand?" White with shock and disbelief,

Amelia pushed the hair out of Sarah's face, then held her close.

"No. But I know I have to." Sarah pulled back and laced her hands together. "I—I just couldn't face it. He'll hate me, I know it. You know how jealous he is of Ben." She shuddered. "What if he thinks I encouraged him? What if he doesn't believe me when I tell him I got away before Ben could—"

The words hung in the air as Amelia considered her friend's words. "Oh, Sarah, he'll believe you. He's learned to trust again these last few weeks. And I'm sure he doesn't blame you anymore. It wasn't your fault."

The front door banged open, and they both turned as Rand, Joel, and Jacob strode into the room. Rand's face brightened as he saw Sarah's scrubbed face and clean hair. "You look much better."

"Well, I'm starved. How 'bout you, honey?" Jacob pulled Amelia to her feet. "Let's go get some grub at the mess hall." They started toward the door. "Come with us, Half-Pint," he told Joel. "We won't be late," he called back over his shoulder.

Sarah yawned hugely as the door banged shut. "I'll fix you some flapjacks," she said, struggling to keep her eyes open.

"Is there anything you'd like to talk about tonight?" Rand's eyes lingered on the livid bruises on her neck and arms. She'd seemed strangely quiet and withdrawn on the trip home.

Sarah sat back down abruptly. She was tired of worrying about his reaction. There was only one way to find out. "Yes, there is," she said slowly.

"Okay. I thought there was something bothering you."

"I haven't told you exactly what happened. I was afraid you'd blame me, but I swear to you I had no idea he would try something like that."

"Who are you talking about?" Rand's voice was puzzled. This wasn't quite what he'd expected.

"Ben. He hired some Laramie loafers to grab me." She blurted the words out in a rush, then hurried on as his face darkened. "When I came to, I was in a locked cabin by myself. Ben showed up—" She drew a ragged breath. "He–he said we should have been married by then. He. . ."

Her words trailed away. Sarah stared at Rand's face fearfully. Would he believe her this time?

"That no-good skunk. So that's what he meant." Rand spoke slowly and precisely. "He gave you those bruises? Did he—did he hurt you in any other way?"

She shook her head, her emerald eyes enormous in her face. " I hit him over the head with a stool leg and knocked him cold. Then I took off and got away while he was out. Labe was there, too, but he wasn't watching the cabin. What did you mean, 'that's what he meant'? When did you talk to him?"

Rand drew a couple of deep breaths, then grabbed his hat.

"Where are you going?"

"To find Jessica. I have some unfinished business to take care of." He came back and kissed her quickly. "Don't go outside the grounds. I might not be lucky enough to find you a second time. Don't look so worried. I'll tell the whole story when I get back." He gazed down into her troubled eyes, then touched her cheek gently. "I know it wasn't your fault, Green Eyes."

She watched him go with some relief. He did trust her after all. "Be careful," she called after his retreating back.

❧

Jessica looked up as her mother ushered Rand into the parlor, then left them alone. "Darling," she said, rising to her feet. "I didn't know you were back." She lifted her face for a kiss, but Rand just stared at her impassively. "What is it? What's wrong?"

"Your little plan failed."

"Whatever do you mean?" Her blue eyes looked huge and innocent.

Rand had never wanted to slap a woman so badly in his

life. "I know all about it, Jessica. Ben told me the whole story when he tried to kill me."

Her eyes widened. "Ben who? Who tried to kill you?"

Rand could see the pulse beating quickly in her throat. She was a smooth one all right, but he could see through her now. "Don't play the innocent with me. You and Ben schemed to kidnap Sarah to get her away from me. You knew I still loved her."

Jessica's face whitened. "How could you prefer that little milksop to me?" she spat. Then her eyes filled with tears. "I love you, Rand. I didn't want to lose you. Surely you can see I had to do something. I could see the hold she had over you."

"I love her. I always have." He saw her flinch but went on anyway. "I tried to deceive myself, but I can't any longer. How could you do such a thing? If people just knew the evil that hides behind that beautiful mask of yours! You can consider our engagement off, of course." He put his hat on and stalked toward the door.

"Wait, Rand!" Jessica ran after him and caught his sleeve. "I know you love me! We can work this out."

He shook her hand off. "All I feel for you is pity." He didn't wait to see the effect of his words but slammed the door behind him.

That was over. Now to find Croftner. He stopped to see Colonel Maynadier, who readily agreed to let him take six men out to look for Ben and try to bring him in.

After two days he had no luck in picking up Ben's trail. Reluctantly, he turned toward Fort Laramie and home. He hated to face Sarah with his failure. He knew neither one of them could rest until they knew the threat Ben posed was eliminated.

He paused atop a bluff, took a swig from his canteen, then led the men down the slope. "Lieutenant, over here!" One of the men waved from the top of the bluff.

Rand trotted over to where the men stood. A body lay face

down in a ravine. He rolled the man over and gasped in shock. It was Labe! Labe groaned. He was alive!

"Get me my canteen," Rand shouted. He poured a little water into Labe's mouth. "Easy, now. Not too much," he cautioned as Labe tried to sit up to suck more water down.

"Indians!" Labe moaned and thrashed around as Rand drew the canteen away.

"They're gone. You're with friends now," Rand said.

"Rand?" Labe peered up at him. "I'm sorry 'bout poor little Sarah. I tried to talk Ben out of it, but he wouldn't listen to no reason."

"Where is Ben?"

Tears welled up in Labe's eyes. "Dead. Indians attacked us. Ben fought them, but he fell off his horse and hit his head. They took his body and buried it over there." He pointed to a long pile of stones.

Rand patted him gently. "How'd you get away?"

"They left me here." He touched his head gingerly. "They must have hit me on the head."

"You'll be all right. We just need to get you back to the fort." He helped Labe to his feet and helped him up into the saddle. It was a long way back to Fort Laramie.

❧

The week flew by as Sarah immersed herself in activity. She tried to still the worry as she thought of Rand out looking for Ben. On Monday, Wednesday, and Friday morning she taught the Indian children. Living with the Sioux for those four days gave her a new love and tenderness for the dark-eyed youngsters who crowded into the small church. She delighted in seeing their solemn faces break into smile.

She had just gotten back from school when Joel came bursting into the parlor. "Rand's back!" She jumped to her feet and followed him out onto the porch where she saw a familiar set of broad shoulders striding toward her across the parade ground. With a cry of relief, she ran into his open arms.

He hugged her tightly, then led her back inside the house. Joel jabbered excitedly as he followed them. "I need to talk to your sister for a few minutes alone, Half-Pint. Can you find something else to do for a little while?"

"Sure. Tommy Justice, the new lieutenant's son, said he'd play baseball with me."

"Thanks." Rand turned back to Sarah. "Sit down here with me. We have a lot to talk about."

Sarah sat down beside him, her heart pounding.

"Ben's dead." He told her what Labe had told him and then the entire story of Ben's plot.

Sarah was surprised at her own reaction. She felt unexplainable sadness over Ben's wasted life, although she knew he had received his just reward. "I read a verse this morning," she began. "It said, 'And he shall bring upon them their own iniquity, and shall cut them off in their own wickedness; yea, the Lord our God shall cut them off.' "

Rand nodded. "But Jessica was in on it, too. And God hasn't cut her off."

"What! She didn't even know Ben."

"The whole thing was her idea." He raked a hand through his hair. "Not that Ben wouldn't have come up with something himself. But the kidnapping was her idea."

"Why would she do such a thing?"

"To get you away from me," he said simply. "She could sense I still had feelings for you." He shook his head. "I had no idea she was capable of such an act of vengeance."

Her heart surged at his admission in spite of her shock. He did still love her! "That's why she left Fort Laramie in such a hurry," she stammered. She saw his questioning look. "She left the day after you did. She's going to Boston with her mother."

"I see." He took a deep breath. "I wanted to tell you at the Sioux encampment, but I felt it was only right that I break things off with Jessica first. I've been a fool, Sarah. I never stopped loving you. I've never loved anyone but you."

She laid a hand on his cheek. "There's fault on both sides," Sarah said softly. "There's nothing to forgive. I've always loved you."

He caught her hand and brought her palm to his lips. "Will you marry me?"

"When?" Her stomach was playing mumblety-peg as he kissed her palm lingeringly.

"Today wouldn't be too soon." He put an arm around her and pulled her onto his lap. "I love you so much, Green Eyes. Even when I told myself I hated you, I knew better deep down." He traced a finger along the curve of her smooth cheek, then bent his head.

As his lips found hers, tears slipped out of Sarah's eyes. She put her arms around his neck as the kiss became more urgent. When he pulled away, she slid her fingers through the rough thatch of his hair.

"Let's not wait too long to marry," he whispered. "I want you all to myself."

"Me, too," she said, blushing. "But what about Joel?"

"He'll live with us, of course. But I think my brother will keep him for a week or so while we settle into married life."

❧

A crisp spring day three days later, Sarah and Rand stood before the post chaplain, Reverend Jameson. Every soldier in the fort had crammed into the tiny church to see their girl decked out in her finery.

In the front pew their families smiled as they watched them say their vows. Joel had been ecstatic when he'd realized he'd get to live with Rand.

After Rand and Sarah repeated their promises, the men behind them put up a rousing cheer as Rand, in his best uniform, kissed Sarah and turned to face the crowd. The officers formed a canopy of swords that he led his bride through and out into the spring sunshine.

Sarah wore her mama's green dress, a perfect match for the emerald eyes she raised to Rand as they clasped hands and stepped out to meet their new life. Her heart had truly led her home.

A Letter To Our Readers

Dear Reader:

In order that we might better contribute to your reading enjoyment, we would appreciate your taking a few minutes to respond to the following questions. When completed, please return to the following:

Rebecca Germany, Managing Editor
Heartsong Presents
PO Box 719
Uhrichsville, Ohio 44683

1. Did you enjoy reading *Where Leads the Heart?*
   ❑ Very much. I would like to see more books
      by this author!
   ❑ Moderately
      I would have enjoyed it more if _____

   _____

2. Are you a member of **Heartsong Presents**? ❑Yes ❑No
   If no, where did you purchase this book?_____

   _____

3. What influenced your decision to purchase this
   book? (Check those that apply.)

   ❑ Cover   ❑ Back cover copy

   ❑ Title   ❑ Friends

   ❑ Publicity   ❑ Other_____

4. How would you rate, on a scale from 1 (poor) to 5
   (superior), the cover design?_____

5. On a scale from 1 (poor) to 10 (superior), please rate the following elements.

    ___Heroine   ___Plot

    ___Hero   ___Inspirational theme

    ___Setting   ___Secondary characters

6. What settings would you like to see covered in **Heartsong Presents** books?_____

7. What are some inspirational themes you would like to see treated in future books?_____

8. Would you be interested in reading other **Heartsong Presents** titles?   ❏ Yes   ❏ No

9. Please check your age range:
   - ❏ Under 18   ❏ 18-24   ❏ 25-34
   - ❏ 35-45   ❏ 46-55   ❏ Over 55

10. How many hours per week do you read? _____

Name _____

Occupation_____

Address_____

City_____ State_____ Zip _____

I Do

A Romantic Collection of Inspirational Novellas

Discover how two words, so softly spoken, create one glorious life with love's bonds unbroken. *I Do*, a collection of four all-new contemporary novellas from **Heartsong Presents** authors, will be available in May 1998. What better way to love than with this collection written especially for those who adore weddings. The book includes *Speak Now or Forever Hold Your Peace* by Veda Boyd Jones, *Once Upon a Dream* by Sally Laity, *Something Old, Something New* by Yvonne Lehman, and *Wrong Church, Wrong Wedding* by Loree Lough. These authors have practically become household names to romance readers, and this collection includes their photos and biographies. (352 pages, Paperbound, 5" x 8")

········· Presents ·········

___HP220 SONG OF THE DOVE, *Peggy Darty*

___HP223 THREADS OF LOVE, *Judith McCoy Miller*

___HP224 EDGE OF DESTINY, *Darlene Mindrup*

___HP227 BRIDGET'S BARGAIN, *Loree Lough*

___HP228 FALLING WATER VALLEY, *Mary Louise Colln*

___HP235 THE LADY ROSE, *Joyce Williams*

___HP236 VALIANT HEART, *Sally Laity*

___HP239 LOGAN'S LADY, *Tracie J. Peterson*

___HP240 THE SUN STILL SHINES, *Linda Ford*

___HP243 THE RISING SUN, *Darlene Mindrup*

___HP244 WOVEN THREADS, *Judith McCoy Miller*

___HP247 STRONG AS THE REDWOOD, *Kristin Billerbeck*

___HP248 RETURN TO TULSA, *Norma Jean Lutz*

___HP251 ESCAPE ON THE WIND, *Jane LaMunyon*

___HP252 ANNA'S HOPE, *Birdie L. Etchison*

___HP255 KATE TIES THE KNOT, *Loree Lough*

___HP256 THE PROMISE OF RAIN, *Sally Krueger*

___HP259 FIVE GEESE FLYING, *Tracie Peterson*

___HP260 THE WILL AND THE WAY, *DeWanna Pace*

___HP263 THE STARFIRE QUILT, *Alice Allen*

___HP264 JOURNEY TOWARD HOME, *Carol Cox*

___HP267 FOR A SONG, *Kathleen Scarth*

___HP268 UNCHAINED HEARTS, *Linda Ford*

___HP271 WHERE LEADS THE HEART, *Colleen Coble*

___HP272 ALBERT'S DESTINY, *Birdie L. Etchison*

Great Inspirational Romance at a Great Price!

Heartsong Presents books are inspirational romances in contemporary and historical settings, designed to give you an enjoyable, spirit-lifting reading experience. You can choose wonderfully written titles from some of today's best authors like Peggy Darty, Sally Laity, Tracie Peterson, Colleen L. Reece, Lauraine Snelling, and many others.

When ordering quantities less than twelve, above titles are $2.95 each.
Not all titles may be available at time of order.

SEND TO: **Heartsong Presents Reader's Service**
P.O. Box 719, Uhrichsville, Ohio 44683

Please send me the items checked above. I am enclosing $_____.
(please add $1.00 to cover postage per order. OH add 6.25% tax. NJ add 6%). Send check or money order, no cash or C.O.D.s, please.
To place a credit card order, call 1-800-847-8270.

NAME _____

ADDRESS _____

CITY/STATE _____ ZIP _____

HPS 4-98

Hearts♥ng Presents
Love Stories Are Rated G!

That's for godly, gratifying, and of course, great! If you love a thrilling love story, but don't appreciate the sordidness of some popular paperback romances, **Heartsong Presents** is for you. In fact, **Heartsong Presents** is the *only inspirational romance book club*, the only one featuring love stories where Christian faith is the primary ingredient in a marriage relationship.

Sign up today to receive your first set of four, never before published Christian romances. Send no money now; you will receive a bill with the first shipment. You may cancel at any time without obligation, and if you aren't completely satisfied with any selection, you may return the books for an immediate refund!

Imagine...four new romances every four weeks—two historical, two contemporary—with men and women like you who long to meet the one God has chosen as the love of their lives...all for the low price of $9.97 postpaid.

To join, simply complete the coupon below and mail to the address provided. **Heartsong Presents** romances are rated G for another reason: They'll arrive *Godspeed!*

*She thought
her true love
was dead.*

Everyone in Wabash, Indiana, is rejoicing in the after-
math of the Civil War—except for Sarah Montgomery.
The war has taken what she held most dear. Receiving
official notification that her fiancé, Rand Campbell, is
dead, Sarah agrees to marry Ben Croftner. But then
Sarah discovers that Rand is alive and that Ben knew
it all along!

Rand returns in time to stop the wedding, but he
is soon to be garrisoned at Fort Laramie in the Dakota
Territory. Eventually, Sarah makes her way to Fort
Laramie only to find that Rand is engaged to another
woman. Sarah has no peace, for she also learns that
Ben has followed her trail to Dakota.

Confined to the tedium of fort life and surrounded
by hostile country, Sarah and Rand must learn that
God is in control even in the midst of circumstances
that try to keep them apart.

*"A man's heart deviseth his way: but the Lord
directeth his steps" (Proverbs 16:9).*

$4.95
ISBN 1-57748-312-X

♥ ♥ ♥ ♥

Historical
Inspirational
Romance

9 781577 483120

DARLENE MINDRUP

A Light
Within